MAR   1996

Other Matt Cobb mysteries

Killed in Fringe Time

A Matt Cobb Mystery

William L. DeAndrea

Simon & Schuster
New York   London   Toronto   Sydney   Tokyo   Singapore

63 13159

SIMON & SCHUSTER
Rockefeller Center
1230 Avenue of the Americas
New York, NY 10020

Designed by Elina D. Nudelman

Manufactured in the United States of America

10 9 8 7 6 5 4 3 2 1

Library of Congress Cataloging-in-Publication Data
DeAndrea, William L.
    Killed in fringe time : a Matt Cobb mystery / William L. DeAndrea.
    p.   cm.
    1. Cobb, Matt (Fictitious character)—Fiction.   2. Television
broadcasting—United States—Employees—Fiction.   I. Title.
PS3554.E174K46   1995
813'.54—dc20
                                                      94-39079
                                                      CIP

0-684-81498-6

To Gregory,
a prime time kid

Killed
in Fringe
Time

A Matt Cobb Mystery

"I hate spunk."
—EDWARD ASNER
The Mary Tyler Moore Show, CBS

1

I am a firm believer in the concept that principles should never be affected by money. I am also a firm believer in the idea that you should always keep two months' rent in the bank, maintain a car length's distance from the car ahead of you for every ten miles per hour on your speedometer, and put Drāno down the sink at least once a week.

Sometimes, though, you don't have any choice.

It was a Friday afternoon at the Network. I was supposed to be working, and I actually sort of was. That is, I was sitting in my chair in my office, holding official Network papers in front of my eyes and in some arcane manner unknown to science but familiar to most people stuck in offices on summer Friday afternoons somehow registering their contents without the actual use of any of my living brain cells.

I was occupying those in marveling at how in love I must be. I was going to give up a weekend in an air-conditioned luxury Central Park West apartment and drive to Maryland with a dog in order to spend Saturday with my girlfriend/lover/partner/inamorata (choose the one that offends you least) in and around a college dormitory, only to have to drive back on Sunday.

Add to this the fact that it was scheduled to be the hottest weekend of the summer, with temperatures virtually guaranteed to top a hundred each day, and my pathological hatred of hot weather and of driving (if they had public transportation in Antarctica, I'd live there) and you can see how the whole project should have filled me with dread.

Only it didn't. Roxanne had been gone for several weeks now, away at this special seminar she'd been chosen for, and I missed her enough not to mind the road or the heat.

Of course, that might change once I got out there and had to start *dealing* with them, but right now, I was very pleased with myself as the very model of the modern boyfriend/lover/partner/etc.

Quarter to four. I was trying to decide whether it was late enough to leave the office and beat some of the traffic. I could leave if I wanted to. As vice president in charge of Special Projects, the youngest VP at the Network, there was nobody to tell me to stay.

But Special Projects is also the smallest department at the Network, and the strangest. We're a euphemistically named bunch of troubleshooters handling everything that's too insecure for security and too private for Public Relations. We depend a lot on teamwork, and if I came on like most of the VPs around the Network, with long lunches and tennis and the rest, I'd probably wreck the rapport that made the department work with a modicum of efficiency and a minimum of nastiness.

And don't doubt for a second that the potential for nastiness is there. People complain about sex and violence on television, but what winds up on the screen is nothing. Television is a world of driven, insecure people who have to keep demonstrating their own existences to themselves with ever-increasing displays of fame or power or wealth or attractiveness.

Well, *everybody* in television isn't like that. Some of us are really wonderful people, once you get to know us. But there's enough of the crazy kind to set the ground rules. If you meet a normal-seeming TV performer or executive, you may assume this person is an island trying to remain afloat on a sea of insanity. You won't often be wrong.

I had just about decided to go the conspicuous virtue route, stick it out until five, and use my good feelings about myself to sustain me during the horrendous traffic jam I would undoubtedly find myself in, when the intercom on my desk buzzed at me.

"Mr. Cobb," came the Cuban-spiced voice of my secretary, Jasmyn Santiago. That meant I had a visitor. We're on a first-name basis in Special Projects except when we have company. "Mr. Cobb, Mr. Bentyne would like—"

I heard another voice, the famous friendly tones of Richard Bentyne. "Like, nothing. I'm going in."

"You *can't*—" Jazz said, and then she took her finger off the button and the connection went.

Now I heard a commotion outside the door. I went to it, pulled it open, and was awarded with a picture the *National Enquirer* would have paid a quarter of a million bucks for: the late-night talk show host the Network had recently given a forty-five-million-dollar contract to about to belt a low-to-mid five-figure-a-year secretary in the mouth.

It was a tableau that had everything. Bentyne was tall and very blond, Jazz a small brown Latina. The only mitigating factor was the fact that Bentyne wore glasses and Jazz didn't.

The glasses did nothing to hide the glint of crazy anger in Bentyne's eyes. Jazz, I think, was cowering away from that as much as from the upraised hand.

And that was where principle gave way to money. I do not care for men who strike women, or even threaten to. I like it even less when the man is big and the woman is small, and the woman is a friend and co-worker of mine.

So what principle called for here was for me to drop this schmuck with a hard shot to the side of the neck, which would have been a snap because of the way he'd been standing and because he only had eyes for his intended target.

Instead, I was given one of my rare flashes of foresight.

It came to me that the company that employed me at a comfortable but still humanly comprehensible sum had just agreed to tie up *forty-five million dollars* for this jerk. With whom would they side in a dispute? No bonus points for getting it on the first guess.

At the very least, I would be fired. Worse, Jazz would be fired.

So I didn't hit him. I darted my hand out and grabbed him by the wrist just as the hand started downward. I gave a hard jerk, and pulled him off-balance. He staggered into my office and across about ten feet of carpeting, but he didn't fall. I decided on balance that I was happy about that, although (in principle) I wouldn't have minded if he'd broken his neck.

I ignored him. "All right, Jazz," I told my secretary. "I'll take care of it from here. Are you all right? Do you want to lodge a complaint? With the Network or the law?"

Her dark eyes were pretty good at flashing anger, too, but apparently she had also been gifted with a flash of foresight. "No, that's all right, Matt. I'll trust you."

"You're sure, now."

She smiled a little. "Chure," she said, "This is the dirty

tricks department, right? We'll think of some way to fix him and keep our jobs at the same time."

"Promise." I looked at my watch. "Look," I said, "it's after four. Why don't you take the rest of the day off?"

Jazz looked dubious. She was one of the most conscientious people I had ever met, and she had ways of making me toe the line as well. In this case, though, I got her to listen to me. She said she'd see me Monday, got her bag, and left. I closed the door behind her.

Richard Bentyne was sitting in my guest's chair, grinning the guileless grin that had charmed millions of late-night TV viewers.

"Excellent, Matt. Really, terrific." You might have thought I'd won the Guess the Punchline contest on his show, and was about to get two free dinners at Gage & Tollner over in Brooklyn. "You've saved me from bad publicity and probably a lawsuit, and you got that harpy the hell out of here. Now all you have to do is give her time to get home, and have someone call her and tell her that as long as she's taking the rest of the day off, she should take the rest of her life off."

I went and sat behind my desk. It's a very impressive piece of furniture, though less so when you find out that all sixty-seven VPs at the Network get identical ebony desks with black marble tops.

As soon as I was seated, Richard Bentyne laced his fingers behind his head and put his feet up on my desk.

I looked at him for a few seconds. All he needed to complete the picture was a big cigar jutting out of his mouth, but Bentyne was a militant, high-profile non-smoker. It was probably the only thing we had in common.

I kept waiting for him to say something, but he just sat there grinning at me.

"What am I supposed to do?" I said. "Read your mind or something?"

"The first thing you're supposed to do is arrange that phone call," he said amicably.

"I'm not arranging any phone calls."

He shrugged. "Or do it yourself, I don't care. But I want that bitch fired."

"You do, huh?"

"Yeah, I do. She laid hands on me in an unfriendly way. I don't like that."

"I didn't exactly caress you."

He grinned. "You were saving me from the tabloids. I'm not unreasonable, you know. I make allowances."

"I'm not unreasonable, either," I told him. "Tell you what. You want my secretary fired. I want Leno and Letterman crushed and broken in the ratings. When you've got that accomplished, then come back and tell me how to run my office. Only that time, wait to be let in. It's called 'manners.' "

"I see," he said without heat. "That's the way you want it, huh?"

"Exactly the way," I told him.

"All right, for now. You'd better hope you stay shacked up with Roxanne Schick forever. Maybe you'd better marry her—then community property . . . is this a community property state? . . . could make you a major stockholder in the Network, too."

"Mmmm," I said. "That would be nice. I could sign your checks, maybe."

Or maybe not, I thought. The first anybody'd heard of Richard Bentyne, he was doing a radio talk show in Waterloo, Iowa. He had a combination of boyishness, brashness, and venom that attracted attention even there.

I say "even there" not to put down Iowa; it's just that late-night talk shows aren't the major format in areas with a lot of agriculture, because too large a percentage of your audience has to go to bed early.

But Bentyne, apparently, was worth staying up for. He

went from there to a daytime half-hour in Chicago, but in the land of Oprah Winfrey, he didn't fit. If Bentyne had a group of abused transvestite pipefitters who were blind in one eye, he wouldn't empathize with them, he'd laugh at them and invite the audience to do the same.

So the Chicago show bit the dust in thirteen weeks, and Bentyne drifted out to L.A., where he did some stand-up (not his best suit), wrote material for other comics, and eventually got his big break, a show on MTV. A talk show on Music Television seems like a contradiction in terms, but only to people who don't know what MTV is really about.

MTV is about being *hip.* This kind of music is *hip.* This kind of movie, these kinds of clothes, this kind of attitude, that political opinion, is *hip.* According to MTV, of course. It's a brilliant thing, really. Teenagers always feel like mutants, anyway, desperate to be accepted on *any* basis, and MTV provided an instant Rosetta Stone of hipness. You didn't even have to read a teen magazine to plug into it, all you needed was cable.

And, of course, the big appeal of *hip* is that it allows you, the former misfit, to join in the snide, patronizing contempt the hip always show to the unhip.

And that was the genius of Richard Bentyne. He'd get on the air, youthful-looking (though he was over forty by now), blond, conservatively dressed, seemingly guileless, and get famous people, from rock stars to politicians, to prove themselves to be utter fools, at the same time demonstrating his own immutable and ineffable hipness.

That hipness had an awful lot to do with cynicism. A rock star once came on the show and said it was no compliment to him that girls he didn't even know wanted to sleep with him because of how well he played his guitar.

That may strike you as rare intelligence among rock stars (it did me, when I saw the tape), but to Bentyne it was the occasion for ten minutes of less-than-subtle sarcasm. It was funny. No denying it was funny. But it was also sort of queasy-making, too.

My opinion was apparently in the minority, especially among executives at the various networks. When Bentyne's contract at MTV was up, they started falling all over each other to give the guy money, bring a fresh jolt of hipness to their channels. This was not entirely due to some adolescent desire on the part of the executives to be *hip*, though I won't deny that was part of it. The major reason they wanted all the *hip* viewers is that in order to be truly *hip*, you've got to spend a lot of money on really useless things. The manufacturers of useless things are assiduous advertisers, and they'll pay a premium to reach the right victims. I mean consumers.

So rich a prize was the man perceived to be that all the networks plus several syndication outfits bid for him. NBC and CBS had already committed their eleven-thirty EST time slots to traditionalist Jay Leno and proto-hipster David Letterman respectively.

Like Letterman before him, Bentyne had his heart (or whatever organ he used for these things) set on the classic, post-local-news time slot, so NBC and CBS were out of it from the beginning. ABC had the prestige news show, *Nightline*. Therefore ABC couldn't guarantee the station clearances, and they were out of the Bentyne sweepstakes.

The syndicators lost out for the same reason. There aren't that many markets with more than three commercial stations in the first place.

That left Fox and us, and we simply offered more money. So we won.

Lucky us.

Bentyne decided to do his show in New York, so the Network bought him a movie theater on Broadway (hey, what the hell, Manhattan real estate is always a good investment) and spent another few million converting it to a TV studio.

And in that studio he was now ensconced, along with an announcer, an orchestra, a staff of writers, and his producer since MTV days, Vivian Pike, who was also his live-in girlfriend.

The show debuted back in May, and while he hadn't replaced Leno or Letterman in the public's affections, he was pulling over twice the ratings of the old movies we'd been showing in that time slot.

At that rate, in the insanely inflated world of TV, the contract would probably turn out to have been a bargain.

But the mood around the Tower of Babble was less than ecstatic. I, thankfully, had not had to do much dealing with Richard Bentyne, and the little exposure I'd had to him (this afternoon, for instance) had done nothing to get his name added to my Christmas card list. Still, the word was that if the man had a saving grace, it was that he really did care about putting on a good show.

In fact, he had ambitions beyond just "good." He wanted to be fresh and innovative as well.

This was a laudable goal. It was also impossible. By the early sixties, Steve Allen and Jack Paar between them had invented every single thing it's possible to do on a TV talk show, from taking guests right off the street to taking the show to exotic locations, to wacky stunts, to working the audience. The only thing that had changed was things were a whole lot raunchier these days. Jack Paar once quit his show because NBC censored a joke about a "water closet."

That seems quaint in an era preschool kids can sit on their mother's laps and watch Phil or Oprah talk to a bunch of homosexuals who have cheated on their lovers with transvestite lesbians, but it was a fact.

Richard Bentyne could tell jokes about water closets *or* homosexuals who had cheated, etc.; in fact he had, scratching his head and wondering if such an act were more perverted or less than what they usually did. Got away with it, too—his lovable/cynical persona somehow placed him outside the bounds of the television religion of Political Correctness.

And so he was rich and free (he had complete control of the show) but he was not happy. Too many of the reviews of his show had said that he was too much like other talk show hosts.

That really scalded him, because in his hipness, he didn't consider himself to be doing a talk show—those were for the rubes. Richard Bentyne was doing a *parody* of talk shows, a satire of them. Stars came on the show to be skewered (which is why so few of them came back); even the audience entered at their own risk.

Anybody *hip* enough count knew that. Except the critics. Unhip though they might be, they still counted, because the press always gets the last word, and they could hurt him.

Which was something very few other people in the world could do. Practically nobody at the Network could, and keep his job. I certainly wasn't among them.

And yet, here he was, having made a special trip over from his Broadway domain to make trouble for me at four-fifteen on a Friday afternoon.

Four-fifteen.

"Hey," I said. "Don't you tape at five-thirty?"

"Sure do. Want to come watch?"

"Watch what? You're over here."

He grinned a little, then put his hand on his chin, sizing me up.

"Well read, Cobb," he said. "Ever do any stand-up?"

"The only public performances I've ever taken part in are basketball games. And not many of them since college."

"Want to come on the show? A Network executive with a sense of humor would be a rarer spectacle than a pregnant panda."

"No thanks," I said.

"Are you sure? It might cost you your job, but it could make you a star."

"Bentyne, I don't even *like* you. Or your show."

"My God, an *honest* Network executive with a sense of humor. Rarer than a pregnant *unicorn*. And you probably wouldn't lose your job at that, not shacked up with the Network's largest single stockholder the way you are."

"You're wasting my time. And yours."

"Don't worry about mine. They can't start without me."

"Why don't you get to the point?"

"The point. Oh yes, the point. The reason I came here, you mean."

I wished there was somebody around to grab my arm so I wouldn't hit him. I restrained myself, but it wasn't easy. He was one of the most irritating humans I'd ever met.

He gave me his trademark chortle. "Actually, I've come to ask you a favor."

"Interesting approach."

"Yeah, well, if I waited to ask favors of people who liked me, I'd never get anything. Nobody likes me. It's part of my charm."

"You come in here, steamroll my secretary, barge in on me, almost hit her, order me to fire her. On top of that, you've got a crew and band and guests and an audience waiting for you at your theater. I've got two questions. Why should anybody like you, and why should I give you so much as a whiff of Limburger, let alone a favor?"

He waved it aside. "Someday I'll do a list of the top-ten reasons people should like me. As for the favor, you won't be doing it for me, personally, you'll be doing it for the show. And therefore, for the Network. That's your job, isn't it? Helping the Network in all sorts of unusual ways? I probably shouldn't have called it a favor at all, but I was being polite."

I had to laugh.

"What's so funny?"

"Your idea of politeness. You got my job description right, I suppose, but part of my job is deciding when something is my job."

He put on a show of thinking hard. "Um, yeah. It's a little complicated, but I think I follow you."

"All right then, what's your problem?" I was silently betting it was death threats or blackmail.

"I need somebody met at the airport," he said.

"To have a heapin' helpin' of their hospitality."
—THEME SONG
The Beverly Hillbillies, CBS

2

And so I was driving through heavy traffic in an
August Friday rush hour, but not to the arms of my beloved. I was on my way to Kennedy International Airport
to meet an eccentric millionaire mountain man.

This job is full of surprises.

Unfortunately, Bentyne had made out a pretty good
case for my doing this. Or he had made up a good story.
I had already promised myself to check it with this Bates
character when his plane got in.

If things checked out, fine. If it turned out that Bentyne
was jerking me around, I'd take up his offer to go on his
show, and I'd tell him a few things. It wouldn't make the
air, of course, but it would make me feel better.

Bentyne had also made me an offer to make the job less

onerous. If I would pick up Clement Bates at Kennedy and drive him up to Connecticut, to Bentyne's recently bought spread in Darien, I could then high-tail it back to White Plains Airport across the state line in Westchester County, New York, hop a flight for Dulles, rent a car, and join my beloved in Bethesda earlier than I would have if I'd been driving. All this was to be charged not to the Network, but to Richard Bentyne, personally.

And, while I admit it was a pleasure to relieve him of some of that forty-five million bucks, that was not the reason I had finally agreed to do it. The reason was that, if Bentyne was telling the truth, Clement Bates *would* be good for the show, and therefore good for the Network.

Sometimes my devotion to my job makes me ill.

I parked at the Northwest Airlines terminal about 7:05. (No, the traffic wasn't *that* bad, I ate in the city before I headed out, planning to have a late snack with Roxanne when I got to her.)

This was just about the time the plane was supposed to be landing, but they never arrive on time. My main worry was that the delay would be interminable, and I wouldn't get to Maryland tonight after all.

Then I went inside, strolled to the arrivals gate, and surprise, surprise. The video monitor informed me that not only was the flight in question not going to be late, it had come in early.

Already, I heard a raspy voice calling, "Bentyne, where are you, you lying bastard? Bentyne? One of his flunkies? What the hell is going on around here when an old man has to stand around confused in a kind of place he's never been before? Bentyne, dammit, if you're out there, show yourself this minute, or I'm going back to Helena and sticking you with the bill."

By this time, airport security was moving in on him. Courts have ruled airports public places, wherein First Amendment rights cannot be impinged upon. That's why you can be buttonholed by Hare Krishnas (freedom of religion) or harangued by LaRouche zombies (freedom of political speech), or buy the world's raunchiest porno (freedom of artistic expression) at airport bookstores.

I myself am a virtual First Amendment Absolutist (I would censor only kiddie porn and writings in praise of the Boston Red Sox), but I've wondered about the porn for sale in airport bookstores. Who buys the stuff? On an airplane, there's nowhere to hide a hard-on. Or a little old lady sits next to you. "What's that you're reading, young man? Oh, how nice, *Oriental Girls with Whips.*" Or what if the plane crashes? When St. Peter asks me what I was doing just before I augured in, I want a better answer than, "I was reading *Teenage Chainsaw Vixens from Outer Space.*"

Anyway, it's because of the fact that it is so hard to tell much of religion, politics, or art from just plain nutsiness these days that you see so many weirdos in airports going unattended to.

Clement Bates (and I was betting that was who it was), though, had apparently been ranting long enough for the guards to decide that this was just an ordinary tirade, and they were about to clear him away.

I moved in just as they were about to grab him.

"Excuse me," I said politely.

I would have guessed his age at about sixty, though I know he was supposed to be a good ten years older. The top of his head came up to my nose. He had bright blue eyes. He was clean, and smelled of lye soap (no mean feat after four hours on a plane), but his blue serge suit and white shirt were too big for him, his string tie looked like the lace off somebody's sneaker, and his coarse gray hair and beard, though short, looked as if they'd been trimmed with an ax.

He lasered me with his eyes. "Who wants to know?"

I produced a business card. There's something ineradicably lower middle class about me that never fails to get a kick out of handing somebody my card.

"Richard Bentyne sent me to meet you."

While he scrutinized the card, possibly for secret messages, one of the security guards said, "Can you keep him under control?"

I said I didn't know, I'd just met him. The other one told me to do my best, and they faded from the scene.

Now Bates was giving me the same scrutiny he'd given the card. "Vice President in Charge of Special Projects," he read. "What's a special project?"

"Oh, running errands for big stars and important guests. Special Projects sounds more important."

"And this Network has a vice president just for that, huh?"

"They have a vice president for everything."

"I thought you seemed awfully young for a vice president," he said.

"Youngest one at the Network. Of course, I hope to work my way up."

"How do I know you're this Matthew Cobb character, anyway?"

I suppressed a sigh and went for my wallet. I showed him my Visa card, my New York State driver's license, and my Network ID, at least two of which had my picture on them.

Once again, he took his time looking them over. "Okay," he said. "You're you. Let's get going."

"Okay," I said. "Where's your bag?"

He held up a small leather thing smaller than the bag my secretary uses for her makeup.

"This Bentyne said he'd get me some clothes while I was here," he explained. "That's one of the reasons I decided to come."

"We're honored," I said. I was amazed to discover that

I kind of meant it. When a man who's shunned the sight of human beings for thirty-five years comes to New York City to be on your show, it *is* an honor.

I led him out to the car, one of the huge black-outside, white-inside gas guzzlers the Network loved. He climbed in, buckled up, and settled into the leather the Network puts on the inside of those ridiculous vehicles.

"This is nice," he said. "Better than the airplane. I might see if I can get a chair like this for my cabin. This is nothing like the taxi I got driven to Helena in, let me tell you. Course, it was nothing like this traffic, either. Never been to New York before. How can you live in a beehive like this."

"We look for a honey," I said.

That, apparently, was a thigh-slapper, though I must admit he did not go so far as to actually slap his thigh. He did laugh for a good long time, so long that it sounded a mite forced.

"A honey," he said, as the laughter trailed away. "That makes everything some easier to take, doesn't it? Course, you get to be my age, used to living alone, and women don't matter so much to you." He tilted his head as though thinking it over. "Am I gonna meet any pretty women when I'm here, Cobb?"

"I thought it didn't matter."

"Doesn't matter *so much*. I may be a hermit, and I may be cracked, but I ain't dead, you know."

"Hold on a second." I paid the toll at the Whitestone Bridge, and headed north through the Bronx toward Connecticut.

"When it comes to meeting women," I told my passenger, "you're on your own. My job description does not include introducing people to women."

Bates let out an impatient gasp. "I never said it did. What the hell do you take me for, Cobb? People want to know why you go off to live by yourself for thirty-five years, that's the reason. Nobody around to go getting you wrong every time you open your darn mouth."

"Sorry," I told him.

"Listen," he went on, "I wasn't born on that mountain, you know. In my day, I met lots of women. Got well acquainted with them, too, and rich as I am, never had to pay a penny, all right?"

"Sure," I told him. "I said I was sorry. Besides, you won't need any help, they'll be all over you. You'll be a challenge to them."

There was just enough light left to see his sly grin. "Yeah, well, you may be right. Bentyne told me the same thing."

"Well, if you want to meet anybody this weekend, you're going to the wrong place. You're staying alone in Bentyne's house while he and his girlfriend hit some parties in the city."

"I know, I know. And that suits me fine. I'm not a fella as plunges right into the stream, you know. Got to dip a toe in first and get some idea how cold it is, and how fast the current's flowing."

We were headed north on 95, which in that part of the country is mostly east.

"Mainly," he said, "I'm going to sit around and eat and watch TV. Get used to human faces again."

It occurred to me that if Bentyne was hooked up with cable, as he undoubtedly was, Bates could get used to a lot more human attributes than just faces, but I didn't tell him. Let him have the fun of discovering for himself.

"So how did you and Bentyne get together?" I asked.

"Didn't he tell you? He said I'd be a legend at that Network of his by the time I got there."

"I was sort of brought into this at the last minute," I temporized. "He's been hinting at a big mystery guest, of a kind we've never seen on television before."

"That's me all right," he said. "You gonna be there at the show, Monday?"

"Probably not."

"Shame. I've been with you almost an hour, now, and I haven't been tempted to slug you but once."

"Oh? Is that another reason you spent all that time up there on the mountain? You go around slugging people when you can reach them?"

"No. It's probably been *fifty* years since I actually hauled off and nailed someone. But when I was going into the office every day, the temptation was horrible. Doesn't this city ever *end?*"

"Oh, we left the New York City limits a while ago. This is New Rochelle."

"You could have fooled me."

"Tell me how you met Bentyne."

"Well, you know, I've got this cabin up in the mountains. I used to go there on weekends, when things got too damn nuts in my office in Helena."

One of the things about me that I don't like too much is that I have a heavy dose of New York snobbery. I am still ashamed of the fact that I dissolved into hysterics when I first heard of the Toledo Philharmonic. I fight it, and most of the time these days, I win.

Therefore, I suppressed any scoffing I might have been inclined to do about a man in Helena, Montana, being overcome with pressure at the office.

It didn't matter. Bates read my mind.

"I'm in the sugar business," he said. "Beet sugar. We grow beets all through here, the Dakotas, Montana, Wyoming, even part of Oregon and Washington. Sell it all through the West. Here in the East, you use cane sugar, grown by foreigners, but our stuff is exactly the same. Do some mining too.

"My granddaddy started the company. Anyway, I'd get away to the cabin, hunt fish, live off the land and L.L.

Bean pancake flour, and one day it came to me that I had *enough money*. Enough to last a dozen lifetimes, especially if I just lived the way I liked to. Know what I mean?"

"I know what you mean. I haven't gotten there yet, but I know what you mean."

That was another thigh-slapper.

When he subsided, he said, "Well, I hope you make it, boy, because doing exactly what you want with your life is a feeling that can't be beat.

"Well, I sold off some of the company to my best assistants, and let them take over the place. They've been running it ever since, and I've got no complaints."

No, I thought, he shouldn't. According to Bentyne, who'd apparently had his business manager check Bates out, the old man was worth a hundred and thirty million bucks and counting.

"I became a real mountain man. It may seem crazy to you, but it suits me fine. You really get to know yourself out there. I'd go years at a time without seeing another human. Before Bentyne showed up, I bet it was oh, nine years at least. When that happens, you get to talk to yourself just to make sure your voice still works, if you know what I mean."

"Yeah. A second ago, you said, 'until Bentyne showed up.' How did he happen to show up?"

Bates grinned. "In a damn fool way, if you really want to know. First of all, he rented a cabin a few mountains away. Told me later he knew he was going to be under almost unimaginable pressure from a bunch of assholes—his word—and that before he started, he wanted to have some time alone and get centered. That was his word, too. Get centered. What the hell was he talking about?"

"Got me. Bentyne didn't know either. That's the big advance in communications since you've been away. We've developed so much jargon that it's possible to

bullshit yourself every bit as thoroughly as you can anybody else."

"Don't kid yourself," the old man told him. "That's
always been the easiest person to fool."

He looked out the window for a while. We'd crossed the
state line, and were cruising along the shore of Long Island Sound in Greenwich.

"The lights are pretty," he observed. "I guess it kind of
makes up for not being able to see the stars."

"If you look off to your right, there, you can see the
Sound."

"Yeah, I see it. Anyway, Bentyne decided to get centered. I told him it was stupid to run away from the pressure *before* you felt it, and then go running back to wallow
in it, but that was what he was doing, and he seemed to
think it was helping him, so I didn't plague him about it."

He gave a little self-deprecating laugh. "What the hell,
when you're a hermit by choice, if you don't believe in
'live and let live,' you don't believe in anything.

"As for what happened, that was the usual city-slicker-
in-the-wilderness story. I won't bore you with a lot of
details. Just one afternoon, he decided to do some 'ex-
ploring.' He made his way over to my mountain, and ex-
plored his way into a twisted ankle.

"He tried to walk for a while, realized he couldn't, and
started yelling for help.

"Well, I heard him. I'd known he was in the cabin—
well, not him personally, but somebody—because I'd been
seeing smoke from the chimney for a couple of days, and
I figured it'd be some damn fool who wouldn't walk down
to the end of his block after dark in the city deciding he
was Daniel Boone out to conquer the Wilderness Trail.

"So I let him yell for a couple of hours—"

"A couple of *hours*?" I had been developing a liking for
my passenger (at least he was different) but this put a

crimp in it. "You left a human being—even if it was Richard Bentyne—screaming in pain and fear for a couple of hours?"

"Yeah, just a couple. I wanted to let the lesson of respecting the wild sink in real good. Tell you the truth, I was hoping somebody else would come along and rescue him. After all, I'd just *had* company, nine years before. I didn't want my place turning into a Hilton Hotel, did I?"

"Oh," I said. "No. Can't have that."

"Course not," he agreed. "Anyway, the afternoon wore on, and nobody came and got him, and he kept yelling and yelling like he couldn't think of anything else to do, and I couldn't leave him there after dark—lot of critters in the mountains hunt by night would go after an injured man, and I knew the idjit didn't have a gun, or he would have been shooting it because gunfire carries a lot farther than a yell. So, eventually, I went and got him.

"I brought him back to my place and gave him water and splinted up his ankle—it wasn't broken, but he had a pretty bad sprain, and we got acquainted.

"He was pretty amused that I didn't know who he was, and apparently he stayed amused for a month, because he stayed right there, telling me all about his life and asking me all about mine, and eating tons of my squirrel and stew and L.L. Bean pancakes.

"And he did go on about this TV show he was starting up in New York come spring. I had to come and be a guest on the show. He even offered to make me a regular. I told him mountain stream water was enough to keep anybody regular, but that was just a joke. There was TV before I took to the cabin, you know, and radio. I know what a 'regular' is.

"I told him the idea was pure nonsense, but he kept coming back to it. I told him I liked him okay, but I'd have to love him like a son to follow him back to New York. Finally, the time came when he had to leave, and he left.

Not to say he wasn't on my tail until the very last second about being on his damned show, but he left. I figured that was the end of him."

"Well," I said, "obviously, he eventually won you over somehow, or you wouldn't be here."

It was dark now. I could only see Bates making a face in the headlights of other cars.

"No, son," he said, "you're wrong there. "The fact is, *I* talked me into it eventually. I was just pottering around out in my cabin, and forgot all about him, really. Then came a day when I figured it had to be May, and I wondered how Bentyne was doing with his show that he'd been so worried about.

"Then I decided, what the hell. So I did something I don't usually do—I wrote somebody a letter. Last time was a writer fella who wanted to write a book about me, or a magazine article or something, but nobody would publish it or give him any money for it unless he got an interview with me. So I wrote back to him. You know what I told him? I told him, *'Good!'* "

He laughed at the memory. "But this time," he went on, "I wrote to Bentyne and told him that though I didn't put much store in such foolishness, I hoped his show was going well. Then I surprised myself. I told him that if he still wanted me on the show, I'd come out and do it.

"I wonder now why I said that. Could it be that I've got such an ego, I want to share my accumulated wisdom of thirty-five years with my fellow citizens? You think it could be that?"

"I don't think there's anything deficient about your ego," I told him.

"No, there is not. There most certainly is not. You can't do what I've done and stick with it and make it work and have anything wrong with your ego."

He shrugged, and leaned back in his seat. "Well, if it turns out to be horrible, I'll just howl for a few hours, then drag myself back to my mountain and never come out again. Meantime, I wrote that letter, left it out on the stump for the postman to pick up, Bentyne got it, wrote back, and here I am."

"And here we are," I said.

"Huh?"

We'd left the highway a while ago. Now I turned off the Fairfield County route onto Richard Bentyne's private drive. The house was a sprawling, modern thing, all glass and stone. Either Bentyne had left the light on for his visitor, or there was a timing gizmo on the electrical system, because the place was lit up like a Christmas tree.

"I thought you said this was in the country," he said. His tone was accusatory.

"Hey, I was born and raised in Manhattan. To me, this is the Amazon."

"Damn it, you can hear the traffic from the road. Listen."

I listened. I heard crickets and an owl and some unidentified rustling in the woods that came up nearly to the house.

When I held my breath, I could hear my heartbeat, and I swear, after a little while of that, I could hear *his* heartbeat.

Finally, I thought I just might possibly have heard a truck go by down the other end of the long, winding driveway, though it might have been the blood roaring in my ears the way it does before you pass out from lack of oxygen.

I let my breath go in a whoosh, and said I was sorry.

"Country," he sneered. "There's gravel on this damned driveway. He kicked some of it, in case I hadn't noticed.

"Look," I told him, "I've got promises to keep. I can take you to a hotel, but it's going to be a whole lot less country than this."

"Oh, hell, I don't mind. This place looks like a tied-down version of your fancy car, there. I just wish people would know what they were talking about."

"Don't we all," I said.

I brought him inside. Bentyne had given me a rough idea of the layout of the place, and I showed Bates around. "Your bedroom, there, bathroom in there—"

We might never have gotten any farther than the bathroom. He kept walking into the shower and looking at its multiple heads. Looking down, he said, "There's one that'll give you a squirt right up the—"

"Yeah." I showed him the Jacuzzi, too, then out to the rest of the house for the air-conditioning controls, the cable and satellite TV, and the vibra-massage lounger in the armchair.

Then out to the kitchen, where I showed him the refrigerator. He stood in front of it, watching it like a movie. There was enough food in it to feed all the starters in the New York Marathon, most of the stuff from Dean & Deluca in the city.

"Well," I told him, "you won't have to shoot anything."

I decided not to try to teach him how the microwave oven worked.

He assured me that he would be all right, and anyway, Bentyne was going to call him in the morning. He thanked me for not being an idjit, and I drove off, expecting never to see him again, except maybe on *The Richard Bentyne Show.*

"Money changes everything."
—CYNDI LAUPER
MTV

3

About seven hours later, Roxanne Schick put her hand on my chest, lifted up her head, shook back her dark hair, then fixed me with her big brown eyes.

"So," she said. "When are we going to get married." I include no question mark because it wasn't exactly a question.

"Don't wince," she said.

"I didn't wince."

"You didn't show a wince, but you thought a wince."

"You're such a mind reader, you tell me."

"The glass is murky," she said. "Like your logic."

"What's that supposed to mean?"

"It means you love me, and you would marry me in a second if I weren't so rich. That's like turning down a limousine as a gift because it has air conditioning. I mean, look at me!"

I looked. She was as beautiful as ever. Almost ever. When I first met her, she was an emaciated teenaged runaway, turning tricks to buy drugs. She was not beautiful then.

Finding her had been a job for Special Projects, and I had done it and was happy about it, but I'd figured it was over when I'd brought her home.

A few years went by, though, and Roxanne got clean, filled out, and grew up. She'd also wised up—a doctor virtually had to threaten her with hospitalization before she'd take so much as an aspirin tablet. When circumstances brought her back into my life, though, she hadn't wised up enough to have gotten over a rather exaggerated regard for me.

Eventually, she'd worn me down and gotten me to admit that, yes, I was in fact crazy about her. Now she was talking marriage.

"It's like the angler fish," I told her.

"The *what?*"

"Angler fish. It's this fish that lives deep below the ocean. It has this little bait gimmick that dangles in front of its mouth, and when some other fish comes and tries to take it, wham, the angler fish scarfs it up."

"What does this have to do with us, Cobb? If you haven't realized it, I've already scarfed you up. I'm just proposing to make it legal."

"No, that's not it. Believe me, no man has ever been better or more happily scarfed." I gave her a kiss and sat up. "See, what everybody thinks of as an angler fish is really the *female* angler fish. The *male* angler fish is about one-hundredth the size. It swims up to the chosen female, and bites with little sharp teeth into her stomach. Eventually, the flesh melds, and he lives off her bloodstream."

"I've heard of couples growing attached," Roxanne dead-panned, "but this is ridiculous."

"Yeah, and they prove the expression two can live as cheaply as one, too, because apparently, she never notices he's there. His only responsibility is to provide sperm on suitable occasions."

Roxanne looked hurt. "Matt, do you honestly think I would make you feel that way?"

"Of course not," I said.

"Good."

"*I* would make me feel that way."

"Men!"

"Have you ever noticed that when women use 'men' as an exclamation, it comes out like a curse, but when men say 'women' it comes out like a cry for help?"

"Never mind that. Get back to the point."

"The point is, when we get married—"

"You said *when*," she pointed out, gleefully.

Mmmm, I thought, so I did. Nice going, subconscious. Well, it (and she) had known I was in love with her before I had, too.

It's weird to be in the middle of an argument and realize you have already lost it, but I pressed on.

"Yeah," I said. "So?" She just looked smug. I went on. "It would be kind of stupid of me to work once I was married to a jillionaire. I mean, it's not like I'm some great artist or something, working for some reason other than to make money. And I certainly couldn't go on working for the Network. Just today, Richard Bentyne was giving me big stondeens about how it was only your being the biggest single stockholder in the Network that was shielding me from his wrath. If I stayed there after we got married, half the people would hate me, and the other half would be afraid of me."

"You could be president of the Network, you know."

"One, I do not want to be president of the goddamn

Network. Secondly, I especially do not want to be president of the goddamn Network by virtue of whom I happen to be sleeping with, okay? Why do you keep bringing that up?"

"I like to watch the way your integrity gets all huffy when you turn me down. Okay, don't run the Network. Quit the Network, and handle my money, instead."

"Roxanne, my darling, have you ever been poor?"

"You know I haven't."

"I have. You wouldn't like it. You just let Mr. Thatcher at the Sloan keep handling your money for you. I can't even balance my checkbook."

"So why do you have to work at all—oh, right, angler fish. Which brings me around to my original question: When *are* we going to get married."

"This is Maryland," I said. "We could rouse a justice of the peace and be married before sunrise."

Her eyes narrowed. "You're bluffing," she said.

"Call me." I was calm as a stagnant pond on the outside. Inside, I was screaming at myself, *What the hell are you doing, you fool?!*

"I'm tempted . . ." she said.

Just then, the phone rang.

Roxanne said an unladylike word. "Who the hell would be calling me here at two-thirty in the morning?" she muttered. She picked up the phone. "Yeah?" she said, then listened for a few seconds, then made a face.

"It's for you," she said. "Harris Brophy."

Great, I thought. Harris is a genial, handsome cynic who is my second in command at Special Projects only because he turned down my job, saying that what he liked about it was amusement without responsibility. He thought the foibles and follies of the rich and famous were the most amusing things imaginable. Had he been less literate, he would have been the perfect *National Enquirer* reader.

"Hail, O leader of persons," he greeted me. "I hope I'm interrupting something worthwhile."

His jovial tone would have encouraged me if I hadn't known that Harris was perfectly capable of laughing at an outbreak of bubonic plague, even if he'd caught it himself.

"Get to the point, Harris."

"Yes. I am calling you from the barracks of the Connecticut State Police in Bridgeport, where your pal Clement Bates is currently incarcerated for discharging an unlicensed firearm into the woods surrounding Richard Bentyne's house. Neighbors complained, the spoilsports."

Wonderful, I thought. I could see headlines. NETWORK GUEST SLAUGHTERS SIX.

"Did he hit anything?"

"Not that we know of. Emptied a six-shooter, though. You should see it. The size of a leg of lamb. Looks like the original Gun That Won the West."

"What was he doing, for God's sake?"

"Repelling invaders. Says they were sneaking up on the house, and wouldn't answer when he called out. So he invited them to eat hot lead. Which meal they declined, according to the cops, if they were ever there in the first place."

"Isn't this a matter for Bentyne's staff?" I said. Now that I realized this wasn't a catastrophe, I was beginning to get irritated.

"Yeah, well, you're the only person from the Network, aside from Bentyne himself, who he's met personally. And," Harris went on accusingly, "you gave him your card."

"That'll teach me."

"Let us hope. Anyway, he tried to get you, got me instead, and here we are."

"So? Get him bailed out, take him home, and stay with

him until you can get him a baby-sitter from Bentyne's staff."

"Naturally. It's already in the works. But first, he wants to talk to you. Nobody's gonna get any peace around here until he does."

Wonderful, I thought again. I wondered if this guy was going to haunt me like a stray dog I'd fed. "Okay, put him on."

Bates must have been standing right there to snatch the phone away from Harris, because the words were hardly out of my mouth before I heard, "Cobb! When can you get up here to straighten these idjits out?"

"I'm not coming up there, Mr. Bates."

"Call me Clem."

I'd been afraid he was going to say that.

"I'm not coming up, Clem. You know how you put good people in place, and took the next thirty-five years off? That's how I handle my weekends. Mr. Brophy is an excellent man, and he can do anything I could do, I promise."

"Hell, he's mostly done it already. That's not the point."

I didn't wait for him to tell me what the point was; I had something I wanted to say.

"Clem," I said. "The next time you get nervous, will you please call the police instead of blasting away?"

He sniffed. "I'm used to being seventy-five miles from the nearest police. Until tonight, I hadn't seen a policeman in—"

"I know, I know, twenty-seven years."

"Twenty-two, actually. Some idjit tourist disappeared or something, and the rangers must have thought I ate him."

"All the same, Clem," I began. You cannot believe the trouble I had bringing myself to call a real human being "Clem."

"All the same, nothing. What do you think about those boys I scared off tonight?"

What did I think? I thought they were undigested traffic noises filtered through an imagination warped by too much time alone. I thought that quaint, funny old Clem Bates was wearing out his welcome with me, really fast. I thought my none-too-potent diplomatic skills were wearing thin.

"Burglars?" I suggested.

Bates made a rude noise in my ear. "I don't believe it. You said yourself, the place was lit up like a Christmas tree."

For a second, I put aside my irritation and did my job. That is, I asked myself to suppose this guy was telling the truth, wasn't just imagining the horrible home invaders.

A second was all it took. Nobody but Bentyne and me, and possibly Harris, depending on whether he'd read the briefing memo I'd left him (he'd swear that he had) knew that it was Clem who was going to be there, with the owner staying in the city.

That meant that whoever was creeping up on the place was expecting to find . . .

"Let me speak to Harris Brophy again."

"Ha! I knew you weren't an idjit."

"No. I'm a genius. Give him the phone."

"I'm back, O mighty one," Harris said.

"Yeah. Get in touch with security. Have them find Bentyne and slap some extra security on him. Just in case our rustic friend is right."

"Will do. See you Monday."

I hung up. Roxanne asked me what it was all about.

"Nothing, I hope." I looked at her, so beautiful and loving and reasonably sane.

"You know," I said, "suddenly getting married to you makes more sense than anything I can think of."

"You mean that?"

"Yeah. I do. Let's go do it."

"No. When we get married, we're going to do it *big*. Soon, but big."

I smiled at her. "However you want it."

"In the meantime, though, there's no reason we can't *act* married."

"No," I said around kisses, "none at all."

"Will he be a *dream?* Or a *dud?*"
—Mystery Date commercial

4

And so we spent the rest of the weekend in what can best be described as bliss, acting married, swimming, eating crabs, acting married some more. I kept realizing at intervals that I had gotten engaged Friday night, and I really liked the idea each time I thought of it.

The only flaw in the gem that was my life was the fear that I'd open a newspaper to read NETWORK STAR KILLED. It didn't happen. Nothing happened. It was the slowest news weekend since the Sunday before God started the Creation. Let me put it this way. A girl with Roxanne's dough would definitely make *The New York Times* with news of her engagement. For all their liberal policies, the *Times* loves people with dough. If we'd announced our engagement *that* weekend, though, it would have made the front page above the fold.

We didn't announce anything. Now that she had me in the bag, she was going to take her time and do everything right. As she pointed out, being an only child, an orphan, and rich, she was going to be able to get everything exactly *her way.*

In that, she was a lot like Richard Bentyne.

I started finding out about that Monday morning, having reluctantly parted with Roxanne and caught the first shuttle back at the crack of dawn. I arrived only a few minutes late, but my secretary had an especially baleful look in her eye.

"Good morning, Jazz," I said.

She made a skeptical noise.

"Look," I told her reasonably. "I'm vice president of this department. I'm paid by results, not by the hour. I don't have to let you bully me all the time about my punctuality. Tell you what—next time I'm late, I'll bring a note from my mother."

"It's not that," she said.

It wasn't? I was astonished. "Oh," I said intelligently. "What is it, Jazz?"

"Mr. Falzet is in your office."

"In *my* office?"

"That's right. He came in person. He had a pot of coffee and two cups on a tray. He asked me very politely if he could go into your office and wait."

That was bad. It was also unprecedented.

Tom Falzet was president of the Network. He was a Southerner, handsome in a big-toothed, horsey kind of way. He was one of the most honest men in the entertainment business, which I grant you is not saying a whole lot, and he did a fine job of running the Network and all its subsidiary activities.

He was also pompous, fussy, narrow-minded, and short-tempered, and I didn't like him.

He, for his part, hated and feared me, mostly because of

my relationship with Roxanne. Virtually all of our meetings took place in his airplane-hangar of an office, in the thirty-seventh-floor penthouse of the Tower of Babble, a place that can make a visitor feel like a Christian crossing the floor of the Coliseum in Rome. I frequently felt that way, especially since I always knew the purpose of my being summoned was to strip some hide off me.

But today, Falzet had decided to play this game on the road. He'd even come bearing gifts. It could mean that he had me so badly, that he could fire me or worse, and not even worry about the stage setting when he did it.

I didn't really believe that. Not only was I not doing anything I could get in trouble for (not always the case in my job), it had been so quiet lately that I wasn't doing much of anything at all.

After that, I was out of ideas, so it was a completely mystified Matt Cobb who walked into his office that day.

I'd half-expected to find Falzet ensconced behind my desk, but he wasn't. He was sitting in the guest's chair, waiting patiently like a good little boy for the principal to arrive.

He stood up when I come in. He didn't say anything about my being late. He didn't sneer. He said, "Sorry to barge in on you like this, Cobb. I took the liberty of bringing some coffee."

It was surreal.

So I acted out of character, too. Instead of asking him exactly what the hell he thought he was pulling, I told him, no, no bother at all. I even thanked him for the coffee, even though coffee gives me heartburn.

He poured. We each fixed our own. He took sugar and cream, and so did I. I waited for him to sip first. Maybe he'd decided to poison me.

He sipped, with no ill effects, so I followed suit. It was good coffee. Maybe during the rest of the year I'd drink eight cups of coffee instead of my usual one cup a month.

"I'll tell you why I dropped in on you, Cobb," he offered.

"I'd like to know," I admitted.

"I received a call this morning, quite early, from Richard Bentyne. In person."

Bentyne had visited me in person; he'd rung Falzet instead of having a flunky do it. This was a guy who needed to learn how to delegate.

"He wanted to know," the president of the Network went on, "why you weren't here personally seeing to his safety. He was very put out."

"Excuse me while I choke back sobs. Did you explain to him that Special Projects isn't in the bodyguard business? That that's Security's job?"

"As a matter of fact, I did."

"Did you further point out that the whole thing was just a precaution, based on the off-chance that an old man who's been talking to himself and the grizzlies for thirty-five years might not be as crazy as he acts?"

"Well, I didn't put it quite that way, but that was the essence of what I'd told him."

"And?"

"And Mr. Bentyne is not impressed with Security. The security department of his last employer failed to deter some demented woman who kept breaking into his home in California, claiming to be his mother."

"I know all about that. Her name is Barbara Anapole, she's out of the nut house in L.A., and she's come to New York. She's stayed away from Bentyne so far, so there's nothing anybody can do."

"Yes, Mr. Bentyne told me all about it. That however was not his point. He is not impressed with Security. He is, it seems, impressed with you. He would like you to spend the day at the theater, to 'keep an eye on things.' " Falzet cleared his throat. "He was quite insistent about it."

"I'll just bet he was. So I go over there today, and nothing happens, possibly because I'm so good at eye-keeping, but probably because nothing was ever going to happen in the first place. What happens tomorrow? I've done a lot of things for this Network, but if I have to become part of a comedian's entourage, I quit."

Falzet looked at me. "What do you think of Richard Bentyne, Cobb?"

"Just between us?" Falzet nodded. "Then I think he's amazing," I said. "I would have bet there wasn't another human being in the world who could irritate me as much as you do, but he's it."

Falzet laughed. It wasn't that I'd never heard him laugh before. But this was different. This wasn't the nasty laugh I knew so well. This one was honest and open and even friendly.

"That's exactly what I would have said if you had asked *me*," he roared.

Now I laughed, although it usually bothers me when people I don't like do something human. Unsettles my prejudices.

"What shall I do with Mr. Bentyne?" he asked.

"Are you really asking me?"

He nodded.

"Well, don't. He's not my responsibility, and I like it that way."

"He seems to want to be your responsibility."

"That," I said, "is his problem."

"Yes, and mine, too. Not that I expect sympathy from you, Cobb. It's just an interesting dilemma. Bentyne represents a huge investment for the Network—larger, in fact, than results have so far justified. We can buy out of the contract, but the kill fee is enormous, not only for him but for his agent, and for that producer/girlfriend of his. More than we can safely afford at this point."

"Count your blessings," I told him. "If he's this snotty now, imagine how bad he would be if he were actually doing what you wanted him to do."

"That's it, Cobb. His ratings and shares have been trending up lately, and of course, his demographics have always been good. He may yet get there. If he does, the income he generates will make him virtually all-powerful at the Network, the way Johnny Carson was able to dictate to NBC."

"Well," I said, "if you're hinting you want me to kill him before he gets too big, you're barking up the wrong tree."

"Must you always be facetious?"

"No," I said.

This brought Falzet up short. He'd been expecting a wisecrack. Now he suspected I'd pulled some kind of double whammy on him and was laughing at him secretly.

He decided to press on.

"I was merely going to point out that it makes good sense for us to, ah, indulge him in any case."

"Humor him, you mean."

"Do I have to remind you, Cobb, that the suggestion that Bentyne might be under threat came originally from you?"

"Actually, it came originally from Bentyne's own private Grizzly Adams, but if it makes you feel any better, I'll admit to buying into it. I wanted to make sure all the bases were covered."

"Exactly. Covering all the bases. If Bentyne does rise to de facto control of the Network, he will be well disposed toward us. If circumstances dictate a parting of the ways, no one will be able to deny we bent over backward to please him."

I formed a mental image of Falzet bending over backward to please Bentyne. Sell a photo of *that* to the *En-*

quirer, and I'd be as rich as my fiancée. That made me decide that I wanted, for my own amusement, a picture of Falzet's face when he learned about Roxanne and me.

It also occurred to me that now I had the answer to Rox's question of the other night. A good time to get married would be as soon as I got sick of working for the Network. After Falzet's speech, that time could be any second now.

But not quite. Not yet.

"All right," I said. "I'll do it—on one condition."

And *there* was the smug, cynical smile I'd always remember him by. "Oh?" he said. "What's that?"

I finished my coffee, put the cup on the tray, and handed it to him.

"Next time," I said, "bring doughnuts, too."

"On with the show, this is it."
—MEL BLANC
The Bugs Bunny Show, ABC

5

Security Guards in New York don't get a lot of respect. Becoming a rent-a-cop is seen as one of those last-resort jobs people in New York take so they can tell themselves they're actors or dancers or writers waiting to happen. Like taxi driver or waitperson, or street-vendor, the other classic tide-you-over jobs, security guarding is flexible enough to leave enough time to go to cattle-call auditions, or to sweet-talk editors.

Unlike them, however, a guard doesn't really get to impress the public with the fast service or snappy patter. He just stands there, checking IDs against names on an approved list, and then says yes or no.

Of course, if you are a *truly devoted* undiscovered superstar, you do the best you can with what you have.

The guy at the door of the Network's newly acquired Bingham Theater, for instance. When we'd bought the place, we'd inherited an ironclad contract with the independent security firm that guarded the place. I'd forgotten about that until I saw the specimen guarding the stage door, now rechristened the Staff Entrance.

I don't know how old he was, but he looked about fourteen. He had red hair and freckles. His two-tone gray uniform was baggy on him, and he made the thirty-eight they'd given him (that was one of the *pluses* of the job—in ten years, every man, woman, and child in New York is going to carry a gun, because the rest will have already been shot) look like a toy simply by being in contact with him.

A casting director might take one look at him and say "Huckleberry Finn," but here that wouldn't work. So Huck did the next best thing. He was small and Irish, so he decided to be Jimmy Cagney.

I took my Network ID out of my wallet, pinned it to my lapel, and let him take a good look at it. Then I said a friendly hello to him, and started to enter.

He jumped in front of me. "Hey, watch it. You can't go in there." He didn't call me a dirty rat, but I could tell he sure wanted to.

I took the card back off my lapel and showed it to him again. "Matthew Cobb," I said, in case the problem here was dyslexia. "*Vice President* Special Projects. See? It"s even got a picture that sort of looks like me."

"It says here," he sneered, "that you work for the Network. It doesn't say anything about *The Richard Bentyne Show.* Nobody goes in here without being part of *The Richard Bentyne Show.*"

This time, he did add, "You get me?"

There were several courses of action open to me, a few of the more tempting of which involved physical violence.

This, however, had been implicitly declared Official Network Bending Over Backward Day, so my voice was sweet reason as I said, "Every day, Mr. Bentyne has new guests. Surely you don't know them all by sight."

Cagneyhuck eyed me suspiciously before admitting truculently, "Of course not."

Still calm as a man talking to a strange dog, I agreed. "Of course not. So how do all these invited guests manage to get in?"

"I call in and check, and somebody comes to get them."

"Wonderful," I said. "Brilliant plan. Would you mind doing that for me?"

"What's your name again?"

"Cobb. Matt Cobb."

He reached into a little box on the wall behind him and got a phone. He cupped a hand around the mouthpiece as though he were reciting the secret of eternal life, or the formula for Coca-Cola, or something equally important.

He folded his arms across his chest and stood against the door. "I called in. It's up to them, now."

"I'll wait," I said sweetly. Inside I was seething with frustration. At the same time, I wondered at the vehemence of my own reaction. The kid was just doing his job, albeit snottily. I decided I was upset because of biorhythms, which I did not believe in, and forgave myself.

Then the door jumped open and he staggered backward into a tall, slim woman. The cigarette in her mouth was crushed against the top of his head, and you could smell hair burning. Cagneyhuck yelped in pain, and staggered forward again through the door, holding his head and looking confused.

"Asshole," the woman said. Her voice said she'd been born bored, and never expected to get over it. She lit another cigarette.

"You're Cobb?" she asked, not impressed.

I admitted it.

"I'm Vivian Pike," she said. The hand she held out was dry and bony, but strong and warm. "Why the hell didn't you walk right in? I've got enough to do without playing doorman for Network busybodies."

"Well, excuse the hell out of me. I was under the impression that Mr. Richard Bentyne desired my presence in the worst way. If I'm wrong, I'll apologize for distracting you, go back to Sixth Avenue, and get on with my real work."

Vivian Pike was about five nine, and rail thin. Her hair was coarse and yellow, and stray bits of it stuck out at odd angles. She was dressed in Early Seventies Graduate Assistant—unbuttoned denim shirt with the sleeves rolled up over a black leotard, jeans, and penny loafers on bare feet.

She was a little older than Richard Bentyne but looked a lot older. It wasn't wrinkles so much as pockets and bulges. She looked unutterably tired. If she'd gotten a little sleep and gained about thirty pounds, she might have been a very attractive woman.

She had pale blue eyes. Now she rolled them heavenward and said, "Christ, another prima donna." She turned to me. "You're the one," she accused, "who put the bug up Richard's ass about his life being in danger, as if I didn't have enough to worry about."

"Just making sure. Old Man Bates might not have been wrapped too tight—"

"My God, *him!* Another one of Richard's brainstorms."

"—but his point just couldn't be ignored. Anyway, what's the big deal about a couple of security men?"

"You don't know Richard." She took a drag on her cigarette as though she expected to live on that lungful of smoke for a week.

"Richard Bentyne," she said, "is a genius. A comic genius. A television genius. He transforms the medium just by being on it. He can be up to his ears in the usual hokey bullshit yet not be touched by it."

Her eyes lit up, as though Richard Bentyne—no, just his talent—were the one thing in the world she cared about. It was just a brief flash of life; it died out as quickly as it came, and her voice was dead again.

"But like a lot of geniuses, Richard is painfully aware of being different, okay? It's made him lonely over his life, and the loneliness has made him paranoid. When he gets paranoid, he gets scared, and when he gets scared he comes running to mama. And it's hard enough just running this show."

She sounded sincerely griped about the whole thing. I would have felt a lot of sympathy for her if I hadn't known that she was shacking up with the paranoid star, and that the Network was paying her a million and three-quarter simoleons a year in salary over and above what Bentyne got personally.

It all went to show that money can't buy happiness, because she sure wasn't happy.

"So you can understand why I don't appreciate having his head filled with hysterical concerns about his safety."

"Yes, ma'am," I said, still on the polite kick. "How would you appreciate it if he got his head blown off?"

She stopped walking and stared at me. "You really think so? You really think this is a serious threat?"

"I really think that Richard Bentyne is an expensive piece of Network livestock on the hoof. Do I really think his life is in danger? No. Am I willing to risk his life and my career—and yours, too, if you think about it, on my opinion? Again, no. Am I willing to humor a paranoid TV genius who thinks I'd be better for him than a highly trained official Network bodyguard? Yes. At least for a little while. Why don't you take me to him, and we can get on with it?"

"Yeah," she said. She took a long, green cigarette out of a cigarette case, stuck it in her mouth, and lit it in continued violation of at least fifty New York City health and fire codes. She sucked on it as if she were starving, and the cigarette her only form of sustenance. She let the smoke ooze out of her, instead of blowing it out. It made it seem as if her head were smoldering.

"Yeah," she said, "let's do that." Her voice and face were as dead as ever, but I thought I caught a flash of respect in her eyes. Some people see the rude as peers and the polite as suckers, and she was obviously one of them. I can play that game, but I don't like it.

She didn't get a chance to lead me there. A production assistant, a young woman in thick glasses wearing a sweatsuit and a California Angels hat backward on her head over thick, straight brown hair, was frowning over her clipboard. She didn't say anything, just sort of stood in the way.

Vivian Pike regarded her with disdain. "What's the trouble, Marcie?"

"One of the props for tonight's show is missing. You know, the flypaper? The prop man's complaining about it. Apparently now it's not in the production cabinet."

"Somebody moved it, Marcie. Ask around."

"I have. Nobody pays attention around here." Marcie had defiant dark eyes, magnified by her glasses. "I'm supposed to be an assistant producer, but I don't get any *respect*."

"Marcie, I've told you, respect from these guys doesn't come with a title. You've got to earn it. You've got to go kick some ass."

"You mean I've got to buy into the patriarchy-established hidden rules of this place? No way. I didn't sue the Network to get this job so I could maintain the status quo. The men around here are defying my authority; as producer it's your job to do something about it."

I was all for more women working at all levels at the Network, although to tell the truth, production staff has always been the one place they weren't underrepresented. Still, I didn't see how it struck a blow against the patriarchy to force your boss to come and bail you out of a situation you couldn't handle yourself.

Vivian Pike grimaced, gave me directions to Bentyne's dressing room, and reminded me I'd better have the secret password for the bodyguard outside. Then she left.

I cheated.

I didn't go directly to Richard Bentyne's dressing room. I hung around awhile and watched a bunch of people go about the business of putting on a TV show. I love TV production—it was the reason I tried to get a job with the Network in the first place. I only got sidetracked into Special Projects because I was young and naive, and somebody in personnel decided that my army service as an MP somehow qualified me for a career of cleaning up after stars and power wielders.

Maybe it did. But it didn't mean I had to like it.

It was good for me to get into a studio every once in a while to remind myself that the ultimate business of the Network was this apparently chaotic bustle of cameramen complaining to unseen technical directors, sound men and lighting men and writers and makeup artists and floor directors, all striving mightily to make the entertainment look effortless.

It's so easy to aggrandize ourselves, to make the Network seem like the hub of the universe. We have to remember that what we actually are is a toy for real people.

I don't get into these philosophical moods too often,

but when I do, I could stand in a blizzard and not notice I was buried in snow.

So it was a good thing something happened to snap me out of it. A man's voice, yelling in anger and fear. What it said was, "You son of a bitch! Are you trying to *kill* me?"

Richard Bentyne's voice. I ran.

"Geez, what a grouch!"
—Danny Thomas
The Danny Thomas Show, CBS

6

Bentyne's dressing room was up a flight of stairs
the entrance to which was behind the permanent desk-
and-couch set. I knocked over an end table and a couple
of people on my way to them. I bounded up the stairs two
at a time, then pushed open a door to find myself staring
down the muzzle of a .38-caliber Hopkins & Allen Police
Positive. It wasn't quite the cannon Clement Bates had let
off in the Connecticut woods the other night, but it was
plenty scary anyway.

I screeched to a stop, eyes for nothing but the gun.

Then the wielder of it said, "Oh, it's you."

I could breathe again. This was Cass Le Boudlier, ex-
Marine, ex–pro football player, six foot four of massive
black muscles from New Orleans. In his other hand, he

held, without effort, a small Hispanic youth in restaurant whites, whom he dangled so that just his toes were touching the floor, which was awash with coffee and littered with ruined pastry and cakes.

The kid, obviously a delivery boy, was terrified, and I couldn't blame him.

"What's going on, Cass?" I asked.

"Damn if I know," Cass said. "Kid come in with the tray from the deli, he brings coffee and cake every day this time, they say. Bentyne says, himself. So I let the kid in. Next thing I know, there's the screaming you must have heard, Bentyne saying the kid wants to kill him, and the kid comes running out through the door. So I grabbed him."

Cass paused a moment and looked hurt. "He spilled coffee all overy my pants, man."

"The Network will spring for the dry cleaning."

"It's not that, Matt. My legs are parboiled, on their way to done."

"Ah. Okay, give me the kid, go run some cold water on yourself, and come back."

"Right." He handed the delivery boy over. I couldn't dangle him the way Cass had, so I left him stand on his feet, and grabbed him around the wrist with one hand and just above the elbow on the other. It's a grip that doesn't hurt in itself, but still gives you total control.

"What's your name?" I asked the kid.

He shook his head, looking more scared than ever. "No spik Eengliss."

I smiled at him. "*Muy bien,*" I told him. "*Yo hablo español.*" I actually speak four languages, counting English, but I don't get much chance to use them, because most of the foreign language speakers I meet want to practice their English.

Young Anibal Cerros, however, had no English to practice, so he was delighted to tell me in Puerto Rican Spanish, the fastest language known to man, that his Uncle Hector would kill him now for messing up the delivery today, the first chance he, Anibal, had had to do it.

But how was he to be blamed? He had gone first to the dressing room of Mr. Bentyne, who was some sort of a big shot, following the written instructions on the list his uncle had given him.

There was a list. I could see it now, wet and translucent in a puddle of coffee.

Anibal chattered on. He brought the order. He put it down, one coffee very dark, one slice chocolate cake. He had turned to go, having been warned to say nothing to Mr. Bentyne, and having no English in any case.

And that was when the yellow-haired man, Mr. Bentyne, had started yelling, *loco*, saying sonovhabeesh, which is one of the few English words Anibal knows, and throwing something at him. Anibal had been afraid, so he ran.

By this time, Cass had returned. I told Anibal to stay with him while I tried to get this straightened out. I promised that no one was going to hurt him, but if he ran away, we would tell his uncle and let him handle it.

Anibal agreed. He seemed to be delighted not to have to go back to the deli and face the music yet.

I went inside, and found Richard Bentyne sitting in an armchair, staring across the room at a polystyrene coffee container and a rather nice-looking piece of devil's food cake as though he expected them to explode.

He looked up from the snack for a split second, just to register my face. "Oh, it's you," he said, and resumed his vigil.

"Yeah," I said. "It's me. At your royal command."

"Leave comedy to the professionals, Cobb. You haven't got the instinct for it."

"Fine," I said. "I'm not feeling too humorous at the moment, anyway. Would you mind telling me what the fuck you think is going on around here?"

"The little bastard tried to kill me. Fat lot of good you or your goddamn bodyguard did me."

"The coffee is poisoned?" I demanded. "Or the cake?"

"The cake."

I went over to the cake. I sniffed it. I picked up a moist crumb on a fingertip and tasted it, then did the same with a few molecules of chocolate frosting.

"There is nothing," I said, "wrong with this cake."

"There is for me," he said bitterly. "I have a gluten allergy, you asshole. Anything made of wheat. If I'd even taken a bite from that, I'd have been hospital material."

"Would you be dead?"

"Probably. If I ate enough."

"I was under the impression you had a piece of chocolate cake every day at this time."

"I do. But not *that* kind of cake. There's a special kind they keep for me, chocolate cake, I mean, made with potato flour, with a fudge icing."

"Sounds yummy," I said.

His voice was rough with hate. "Oh, yeah, Cobb, yuk it up. Do you know what a bitch it is having to go through life avoiding *wheat*?"

"I don't know. Just hanging around you makes me see the humor in the misfortunes of others. What happens to you when you eat this stuff?"

"Hives. Asthma. Respiratory arrest, if I eat enough."

"Would you die?"

"If you don't breathe, you die, Cobb. Didn't you ever take high school biology? Maybe I should save it for my last show—how many slices of bread can Bentyne eat before he snuffs it? Later the Network can sell the video."

By then, I was about ready to buy a copy. As Red Skelton said at the funeral of Harry Cohn, "Just give the public what it wants . . ."

"Let me ask you a few questions," I said.

"I'm trying to do a show here."

"You sent for me, you're struck with me."

"Oh," he groaned petulantly, "get it over with."

"Glad to," I said. "Now, did you eat any of the cake that's here?"

"Of course not."

"I don't see any of course about it. How did you know not to?"

"You can tell by looking at it. This is devil's food cake, you can see it's kind of red-brown. The stuff I get is more the color of chocolate milk. And then there's the texture. The wheatless cake doesn't have crumbs like this, it's more grainy, looks almost like marzipan."

"Then there's no chance you would have eaten any of this," I said.

"Goddamnit, Cobb, what does it take to get it through your head? That stuff is *poison* to me!"

"So the Puerto Rican kid outside, first day on the job, grabbed the wrong cake, and you decided to have a tantrum about it."

"How much is the Puerto Rican kid worth to your girlfriend's Network, Cobb?" he sneered.

I looked at him for a long time.

"You are pathetic," I said at last. "Are you really so worthless in your own estimation that you've got to pick on a harmless kid to dramatize yourself?"

Bentyne turned purple, on his way to black. I was expecting an explosion. I was already rehearsing how I was going to explain to Falzet that though he'd sent me over to humor Bentyne, what I'd wound up doing was driving him off the show instead.

Then a strange thing happened. He got control of himself. The color drained out of his face until he was damned near white. Finally, he whispered, "Is it that obvious?"

"To anybody four years old and up who thinks about it for two minutes. Most of them don't want to think about it, because they see you as a cash cow, and they want to believe you'll provide decades of healthy milk-ings."

"How are you different?"

"Me? I just don't give a shit. I learned a long time ago that people who hate themselves are the most dangerous animals on the planet."

"I don't hate myself," he said.

"No?" I shrugged. "Suit yourself. You give a damned good imitation of it. The key thing is the assumption that anybody who actually *likes* someone like you is either fak-ing it, or such an asshole that they deserve whatever you can do to them, right?"

"I don't!" he yelled. "Hate myself, I mean." He strug-gled helplessly for a few seconds, as if looking for a word.

"It's just like," he went on at last, "I don't see what there is to *like*."

He'd leaned way forward in his armchair. Now he plopped back into it in a state of total collapse. "I was a nerd all my life. The people who didn't laugh at me, ignored me completely. Then in college, it changed. Peo-ple started laughing at my jokes, and throwing money at me for telling them. The nastier they got, the more they loved me. And it's still true. People *want* me to insult them, I've been chosen to bring nastiness and insults into their lives."

Absentmindedly, he messed up his carefully combed blond hair with his hand. "If I could understand it, I could deal with it better. But I don't understand it, and I never will."

He leaned forward again. "But I'll tell you one thing, Cobb. I'm not going back. It's better to be rich than poor. It's better to be feared than despised, and it's better to be hated than ignored."

"Bullshit," I said. "Fine. You've got a nasty comedy persona and it pays off for you. Why don't you try to save it for the camera? Because you're going to lose everything but the money eventually."

"When did you hang up a shingle?" There was the trace of a sneer; he was rapidly getting back to what passed for normal.

"I don't have to hang up a shingle, that's what I'm trying to tell you. Step back and take a look at Vivian Pike."

"What about her?"

"I've only spent a couple of minutes with her, but I can see she's a woman on the verge of burnout."

"Well," he said pulling his lip, "at least she's giving herself in a good cause."

"So you're stupid as well as neurotic," I said.

"What's that supposed to mean?"

"It means that one of these days, she'll get sick of you, and when she does, she'll be in a position to squash you."

He waved it off. "We've both been under a lot of pressure lately."

"Yeah. Maybe you'd better go twist your leg up in the mountains, again. Clement Bates seems to be the only human being on earth you haven't alienated yet."

His face lit up. "Bates!" he said. "How is the old bastard? Has he come to the studio yet?"

I'd seen his name checked off on the redheaded gatekeeper's list. "He's here," I said. "I haven't seen him personally. I've been chasing false alarms."

"Go see if he's all right," Bentyne commanded. "That's really the kind of thing I wanted you here for today."

I thought of seven thousand, five hundred forty-three suitable responses, but since none of them would do any good, I shelved them. I reached for the door.

Behind me, Bentyne said, "Cobb?" I turned. "Thanks for all your help," he said. "I really mean it."

"Name your poison, mister."
—GLENN STRANGE
Gunsmoke, CBS

7

I got things straightened out in the hallway, told
Anibal he could go back to the diner, and not to worry. I
suggested that Cass personally take any deliveries to Bentyne's dressing room, and bring them in himself. Somehow, I didn't think Bentyne would try to intimidate Cass
the way he had the delivery boy.

The next thing to do was to look up Vivian Pike. She
had somehow come to grips with the Marcie situation. I
could see a happy Marcie lording it over a stagehand who'd
probably been at the Network since before she was born.

Vivian Pike, it was safe to say, did not look happy. I
approached her, since glum as she was she seemed to be
the only sane one in the place.

I started to ask her where Bates was hiding when she cut
me off.

"The flypaper turned up. A few sheets missing. What do you think of our little Marcie?" she asked.

I made a face. "Do I have to?"

"Have to what? Tell me?"

"No. Think about her. That kind of person always makes me depressed."

She gave a tired simulation of a laugh. "Me, too."

"You do seem to be knee-deep in them."

She looked at me for a second through a haze of smoke. "Oh," she said. "You mean Richard. No, there's no similarity between them. Richard's a spoiled child. Marcie's a barracuda."

"What the hell," I said. "You're the producer, aren't you? If you can't fire her, and you probably can't given the lawsuit, get her moved to another show. You've probably got enough juice to get her *promoted* to another show. Then she couldn't complain of discrimination, and you'd have her out of your hair."

"It's a good idea," Vivian Pike conceded. "Only one problem with it."

"What's that?"

"Richard is fucking her."

"Oh," I said. "You appear to be taking it calmly."

"Who me? I take everything calmly. That's why God gave us Valium."

She took another deep drag on her cigarette, and it occurred to me that tobacco and prescription tranquilizers were two of the unhippest drugs around these days. I was surprised using them didn't disqualify her from the show.

"Besides," she continued, "I only live with the man, I don't own him. The spirit of tomorrow, you know? I happen to know that Marcie has a bitchin' bod, as we say in California, under that sweatsuit, so what the hell? We're liberated, we're free, we're— Oh, you know the rest of the bullshit as well as I do."

She took another deep drag and added under her

breath, "Besides, the bastard never touches me anymore, anyway." In a louder voice, she said, "What can I do for you?"

The juxtaposition was suggestive, but she probably didn't mean it, and even if she did, I wasn't having any.

It occurred to me that she might have taken a little extra Valium today, and that her mouth was loosening up along with her nerves, but I kept the observation to myself, and asked her where I might find Clement Bates.

"Oh, good," she said. "Go keep the loony busy before he starts shooting at pigeons in the rafters. You know what I think?" she said.

I bit. "What?"

"I think the Mountain Man is going to wimp out. He's already hiding from the production crew. He's going to come out on stage, see the audience, and shit his buckskin pants, won't say a word on the air, and I'll be a laughing-stock in all tomorrow's papers."

"Maybe you should slip him a Valium."

"Up his. I'll need all I've got." She told me where to find him, and off I went.

Because he'd shown up so early (most of the guests would show up about an hour before the 5:30 P.M. taping time, although a real big star could walk right off the street and be led directly to the couch), Clement Bates had not been ensconced in the mysteriously named Green Room, none of which is ever green, and had been given a dressing room of his own, as if he were Madonna or somebody.

Well, not exactly. There was no glittering star on his door, just the prosaic figures B13 badly stenciled in white on a dark green metal door, the kind that makes a bloop-ing sound when you knock on it.

The voice I had grown to know Friday evening said, "Who is it? What do you want?"

I had visions of him with his goddamn pistol in there. It

probably hadn't occurred to him to leave it up in Connecticut.

"It's me," I said ungrammatically. "Matt Cobb. I drove you to Bentyne's house the other night."

The door creaked open, and the familiar bearded face greeted me. "Come on in," it said. "I know who you are, cripes, it was only three days ago. You'd think I was senile or something."

"Richard Bentyne asked me to come over here and make sure you were okay," I said. It wasn't exactly a lie.

"I'm fine. That him yelling before?"

"That was him, all right."

"I thought so. Ain't doing so well, is he?"

Since there was nothing I could do with that one except agree with it, I ignored it.

"He says he'll be around to see you when he gets the chance."

Bates snorted. "Tell him to forget it until he gets his attitude in order. Otherwise, I ain't interested."

"You're going to have to talk to him on the air, you know," I warned him.

"On the air is different. I agreed to do that, and I stick by my word. Besides, he's got to be more in control on the air."

"How do you know?" I demanded. "Up till Friday night, you hadn't seen any television in thirty-five years."

He looked for a second as if he were going to be angry with me, then decided against it.

"Yeah," he said, "but I sure got an eyeful Friday night. Including Bentyne's show, by the way. Besides, it stands to reason. If he was as nuts in front of millions of viewers every night as I've heard him being in this building this morning, he would have been locked away a long time ago."

He scratched his beard. "Looking back, I'm a little ner-

vous at the idea of having spent a month under the same
roof as him. Though, to be fair, he was as nice as pie."

"You were lucky," I told him. "It could have been like
shacking up with Sybil."

And with that, I did it again. Bates cracked up and kept
laughing long past what I thought the gag was worth.
Finally he calmed down enough to say. "Yessir. Boy, am I
glad I got the friendly personality."

"Yeah," I said, "especially since you're the only one who
has."

He started to wheeze into another laughing fit, but he
and I were saved by a knock at the door.

"You get it, Cobb," he told me. "I've got to go to the
jakes for a while." He picked up an old issue of *Mirabella*
magazine, whether to read or to substitute for a primary
function of the now-defunct Sears Roebuck catalog in his
neck of the woods, I couldn't say.

I got up and answered the door. Outside was a tall guy,
maybe six five or six six. He was bald with a black fringe,
and he wore gray-framed half-glasses on the bridge of a
hooked nose. He wore gray slacks, a white shirt, and a
blue-checked bow tie. He looked like a small-town high
school principal.

"Yes?" I said.

"Well, now. You're not Clement Bates, are you?"

"Neither are you," I informed him. I pointed to my
badge, which I hated. I feel stupid wearing a picture of my
own face on my lapel. "Matt Cobb," I said. "Network
Special Projects. Bentyne wants me here. Your turn."

"We've got the wrong faces, don't we?" he offered. "I
mean, I look much more like what people think a Network
vice president ought to look like, don't you think? Not
that you look like a comedy writer. At least what I'd like to
imagine a comedy writer looks like."

"You're a comedy writer," I deduced.

"Oh, right, right. Alf Kriecz." He stuck out a hand for me to shake. It felt like a bag of candy canes, but his grip was strong enough. "I'm head writer on the show. Used to write for Carson, at the very end."

There was something wrong about this guy. Too deferential. In appearance, the classic nerd. I refused to believe it was for real. After all, the essence of Bentyne's humor was the put-on, the continued kidding of the unhip. Maybe to be head writer for the guy you had to devote your life to it or something.

"Maybe that's why he retired."

Kriecz opened his mouth and eyes in a look of delight. He pulled a small notebook and the stub of a pencil from a hip pocket. "That's good, he said scribbling. "That's very good. Don't be surprised if we use that one sometime, Mr. Cobb. And no royalties for you, either."

All right, now I knew. My putdown had been a test, and Alf Kriecz had failed it. If he were what he'd been pretending to be, it would have hurt him or, more likely, made him laugh a little, or most likely, had him come back with a topper.

So he was putting me on, and no doubt intended to put Bates on. He probably put on everybody who walked into the studio except for the anointed *hip*. No wonder the word in the industry was that Vivian Pike had had to up her Valium intake because of the fact that it was so hard to get name guests to submit themselves to the Bentyne treatment.

As a (very) minor stockholder in the Network, I was beginning to think that the forty-five million bucks was going to turn out to be a waste of money, but I had to remind myself that the only thing that mattered was what went out over the air. The fact that there were millions of young Americans out there who described themselves as "the Richard Bentyne Generation" was good news for my investment, however big a tragedy it might be for the country.

I was about to ask Kriecz how I could help him (a swift kick in the ass sprang to mind) when a toilet flushed as loud as a space shuttle launch, and Clement Bates appeared, hitching up his pants.

He looked up at Kriecz, rubbed his beard, and said, "By Jesus, I've *heard* of people growing up through the top of their hair, but I never thought I'd see it."

Kriecz stood there.

"Write that one in the notebook," I suggested helpfully.

To give him credit, he did it. I guess if your life is an imposture, if you don't stick with it, you don't have any life at all.

I pronounced names. Bates said. "Writer? What can I do for you, sonny?"

Kriecz explained that he and the writing staff had prepared some possible answers for questions Richard might be asking him during the taping.

"Some guests, especially if they're new to television, tend to tense up with the lights and the crowd. We like to have the guest ready in those situations, give him something to fall back on. Richard understands; we've got questions written for him that will tie into these answers beautifully. You'll look like a genius."

The contempt behind the ingratiating grin was so strong, you could almost smell it. I looked at my watch. Eleven-fifty. I'd only been here an hour and a half. It felt like eternity. The only people I'd spoken to this morning who I could even stand were Bates and Vivian Pike, and they wouldn't be my first choices to be trapped in an elevator with, either.

I was beginning to get an idea of what hell must be like. This studio, forever.

Bates sat down and told Kriecz to do the same. There were no chairs left, so the writer perched on the edge of a makeup table.

"Let me get this straight," the guest said. "You've written down a bunch of stuff for me to say? And I go out there and say it?"

"Well, if you have to. But yes, that's basically it."

The beard bristled.

"Stand up!" Bates demanded.

Kriecz looked astonished. This time, it was no put-on. "What?"

"I said stand up. I'm going to paste you one, and you can't hit a man while he's sitting down. Stand up, dammit!"

"What's the matter with you?" Getting no answer, Kriecz tried the question on me. "What's the matter with him?"

"Maybe he likes to speak for himself," I suggested.

"You're damned right!" Bates yelled. "I didn't come any two thousand miles just to parrot the words of some slick New York hack who thinks he knows how to make me funny. I didn't come here to be funny! I came here to be myself! I may be a hermit, but I'm no goddamn *rube. I've got over a hundred million dollars*, you idjit!"

He walked over to the still-seated Kriecz but did not paste him one.

"Does Bentyne know you're doing this? I don't think so, because while he may be crazy, he ain't stupid. But if he did know, I'm walking out of here right now. I don't need him, I don't need the show, and I certainly don't need you."

"Um . . . Richard doesn't know anything about it. About you specifically, I mean. It's just a routine. A routine thing that we do. To, um, make it easier. For the guests."

Bates poked each word home with an index finger to Kriecz's chest. "I ain't no routine guest."

He took a breath. "Okay, I'll stay for now. But no more insults. And I don't want to see your smirking face around at all."

"Um, right." Kriecz and his smirking face made themselves scarce.

Bates waited until the door clicked closed.

"People," he spat. "They bring out the worst in me. Listen, Cobb, as long as you're here, I need your help with a little problem I'm having."

I suppressed a sigh. "What's that?"

"Those idjit cops up in Connecticut took my gun and won't give it back."

I managed not to actually cheer out loud. I was about to explain how these things could take a *long, long* time, when there was a banging on the door that sounded as if it would leave dents in the metal.

It was Vivian Pike. She was breathless and sobbing. Something had gotten past the Valium.

"Cobb," she said, "come quick! Richard is terribly sick, and he's calling for you."

"Bon appétit!"
—JULIA CHILD
The French Chef, PBS

8

By the time I got there, he was no longer calling my name, mostly because he was throwing up, writhing, turning colors, and all the other things poisoned people do before they die.

"All right," I said, exactly like a man who knew what he was doing. "All right," I said again, and finally my brain started to work.

My first thought had been that Bentyne had yielded to temptation, and had scarfed down the forbidden chocolate cake, but a quick glance around the room showed it on the makeup table where it had always been, sitting there like Exhibit A.

What had been eaten in that room recently was chicken. Fried chicken, to be precise. There were chicken bones in the garbage can, and brown crumbs in the folds of a crumpled napkin on a round table. There was also an empty pilsner glass with traces of foam clinging to it, and an empty Grolsch bottle, the kind with the built-in stopper, leading me to deduce Bentyne had drunk beer, too.

It was obvious that something he had eaten had disagreed with him mightily. Bentyne was twitching now; I bent to hold him still. He was clammy and hot.

I looked up to see faces floating like bubbles in the doorway.

I recognized a couple. "Cass," I said.

"Yo!"

"Visit all the security guards. Nobody leaves the building. Get the names of anybody who has left the place in the last hour or so."

There was finally emotion in Vivian Pike's voice. She said, "Are you trying to say—"

"I'm not trying, I'm saying it. You call 911. Say we've got what looks like an acute case of heavy metal poisoning, and we need an ambulance and the cops."

Marcie clicked her tongue in impatience. "He's obviously *dying*," she said, as if it needed to be pointed out. "I think you should—"

"Nobody gives a shit what you think!" I snapped. Boy, did that feel good. "You want to accomplish anything, all of you try to remember if you noticed who gave him the chicken."

There was a general murmur. An unidentified voice from the back of the crowd said, "The black guy gave him the chicken. Your security man."

There is a phenomenon known as a klong, a term described by its coiner, political pro Frank Mankiewicz as "a sudden rush of shit to the heart."

I experienced a klong just then, with the realization that I might have just sent a murderer to run away and lock up after himself like a good boy.

Fortunately, I didn't have long to agonize over it, because a few seconds later Cass was back. If he wondered
why the crowd parted around him like the Red Sea, he
didn't let on.

"All set, Matt," he said.

"It looks like he was poisoned with the chicken or the
beer, Cass."

"Really?" Cass said. He found the matter merely of
academic interest. "Well, I got a list of suspects for you,
then. Or I will have. People been in and out of here like a
public toilet since Gambrelli delivered the basket."

"Gambrelli?"

"Network chauffeur assigned to the show," Vivian
Pike said. I hadn't noticed her return. "He brings Richard's lunch in from Darien every day about eleven-
thirty." Vivian Pike looked at me and answered the
question I was about to ask. "Ambulance and cops on
their way."

There was a question in her face, too—"How is he?"
but I ignored it because she wouldn't like the answer.

Richard Bentyne was dying under my hands. If the ambulance showed up this second, it would be too late. If we
could somehow teleport him this second to the emergency
room of Columbia Presbyterian Medical Center, it would
still be too late.

As usual, the cops got there before the ambulance did—
their cars are smaller, and there are more of them. One of
the cops, a grizzled veteran with about five citations
pinned under his shield, took one look at Bentyne and told
his partner to get back to the radio and call for the medical
examiner and homicide.

Vivian Pike gave a little-girlish shriek, the last thing I
would have expected from her. From Marcie, we got exactly what I would have expected—abuse. "You haven't
even done anything. Why don't you ask questions? Why

don't you help Richard? Typical men—hog all the power, deny any responsibility."

She was unanimously ignored.

The cop, on the other hand, narrowed his eyes at me. "You're Cobb, right? Matt Cobb?"

"Yeah," I said. "I am. Do I know you?"

He gave me a small grin. "No, but I know you by reputation"—he lifted his head and called to his retreating partner. "Reynolds! When you call homicide, ask for Lieutenant Martin."

And twenty minutes later, Lieutenant Martin it was. Now that my own dad's gone, Detective Lieutenant Cornelius U. Martin Jr. was the closest thing I had to a father figure. And a big figure he is, too; massive and brown, with a frosting of white hair on top, his nickname on the force was the Chocolate Mountain. Despite his protests, he secretly liked it.

Mr. M and his family had integrated our building when I was a kid, and his son, Cornelius III, and I had grown up together, sneaking up to Harlem to play in the toughest basketball games we could find. It had paid off for us. I'd won a scholarship to an expensive college I'd never have been able to afford otherwise, and Corny had ridden his talents through a University of North Carolina degree and a lucrative, if injury-shortened career in the NBA. He was happily coaching in the Midwest.

And his father was still chasing murderers in New York.

Lieutenant Martin grunted when he saw me. He was accompanied, as always, by Detective First Grade Horace Rivetz, a balding, wiry guy who seemed as hard as his name.

Usually. Today, he seemed out of sorts and subdued. When Martin told him to take names among the crowd while Martin interviewed me as his first witness, Rivetz let me go by without so much as a sneer, let alone a sarcastic remark. He simply gave me a mild, "Hello, Cobb," then ignored me and turned to his work.

While Rivetz and the rest of the team got on with it, Mr. M led me away. When we were out of earshot, he said, "Where can we talk? You'll have to fill me in on the background here."

"You trust me too much," I told him. "One of these days, I'm going to turn out to be the one who did it, and I can fill your head with lies."

"Don't even joke about it, Matty. Anybody can get tempted to kill somebody. You for instance. I should have snuffed your candle when I had the chance, before you got them all convinced downtown that I'm some kind of TV murder specialist. I don't even watch TV."

"Mmm hmm," I said.

"Except for sports."

"Right."

"And the old *Dick Van Dyke Show* on Nick at Nite. But that's it. I sure don't watch much on this Network, despite all the cases you arrange for me around here. How much do they charge you for insurance, working for this place? Whatever it is, I bet they're losing money."

I brought him to Bates's dressing room, knocked on the door, and brought him inside.

"Bates," I said.

"Clem."

Okay, I told myself, it was the guy's name. If society could get used to taking names like Prince and Madonna and Arthur Garfunkel for granted, I could get used to the idea of somebody out of an old Disney cartoon named Clem.

"All right, Clem. Listen—"

"And I'll call you Matt. What's all the commotion?"

"Something's happened to Bentyne. This is Lieutenant

Martin of the New York Police Department. He's going to want to talk to you in a little while. In the—"

"Police?" Bates said. "You mean Bentyne got somebody mad enough to thump him?"

"Not exactly. I—"

"Well, it must be something, if the police are here." He turned to Martin. "Pleased to meet you, by the way, I'm Clement Bates. Nobody beat him up?"

"No," I said. I looked at Lieutenant Martin. He nodded. "Bentyne's dead," I said.

Bates's eyes and mouth opened wide. "They got him," he said.

Mr. M was beginning to look exasperated. "Just a minute," he demanded. "*Who* got him?"

"Well, bless me, Lieutenant, how the hell should *I* know? Whoever I scared off Friday. I didn't see them too good. How'd they do it? I didn't hear any shots, but this is a funny old building with heavy doors, and I might not have. So what can I do for you?"

The lieutenant said, "Huh?"

"Well, I assume you've come to me because you want my help in catching the bastards, right? I'm the only one who's had anything to do with them after all, even if they were just shadowy figures in the dark. Who do we question first?"

I decided I'd better do something about this situation right away, or Lieutenant Martin really would shoot me.

"Oh, that comes later, um, Clem. For now, the lieutenant is going to hand you over to one of his detectives, and you can brief him."

"Her," the lieutenant said. He opened the door and said, "Hernandez!" A young woman with nice black eyes a lot like Roxanne's came up to the door. "Yeah, Lieutenant?"

"This is Mr. Bates. Find a place to talk with him, see

what he can tell you. He's a background witness." Now the lieutenant looked at me, and I nodded. "Come back here when Hernandez is through with you," Martin told Bates.

"Sure thing, Lieutenant."

They left. Mr. M's face clouded up in a scowl. "You're doing it to me again, boy."

I asked him what he meant.

"Pulled me in on some lunatic case. Bates is a background witness? To what? The Alamo?"

The only thing to do at that point was to fill him in, fully. I did so, right up to the little visit with Kriecz, and Marcie's dissatisfaction with our efforts over the soon-to-be-clay of Richard Bentyne.

It failed to cheer him up.

"Now, you're going to try to persuade me that this isn't a madhouse, right?"

"Somebody'd have to persuade me, first. It looks like a pipe dream to me."

"Yeah," he growled, "well, one thing's not a pipe dream. That stiff up there isn't a pipe dream. He's about the deadest SOB I ever saw. You told the cop heavy metal poisoning. You know something?"

I shook my head. "I just read a lot. After Lenny Green got murdered in front of us, I went through a phase of being morbidly curious about poisons. This fit the symptoms. The bitch of it is that I had a bodyguard right outside his door, and Bentyne got the chop anyway."

"We're going to have to check your bodyguard out."

"Of course. But he'll check out fine. He's been with the Network for years."

"Which doesn't mean he doesn't suddenly need money and arrange to turn the other way when somebody sneaks in some arsenic-laced chicken."

"You sure it was the chicken?" I asked.

"Sure," he said. "Assuming you're right about it's being arsenic. It's a long time since I took toxicology, but I remember enough to know that. Acute arsenic poisoning rarely takes longer than an hour or so to polish off the victim. Of course, there's cumulative arsenic poisoning, smaller doses over time, but that tends to look like a progressive disease. Right, Mr. Morbidly Curious?"

"Yep," I said, "absolutely. But that wasn't what I was talking about. I mean we know the poison wasn't in the beer—again, if it was arsenic. It doesn't dissolve in liquid that way, and beer is nice and clear—too easy to see the flakes in it. And we know the chicken was the last thing he ate. Hell, I think he had some in his mouth when I got there."

"Yeah?"

"The question is, did he eat anything *before* the chicken?"

The lieutenant shrugged. "The lab boys will tell us about that. And if anybody around here knows anything about it, Rivetz will dig it up."

He paused for a moment and scowled. "Maybe I better go see how Rivetz is doing."

This was unprecedented. Rivetz was a thirty-year man, and a detective first (who makes more money than a sergeant) on top of it. He'd never been Mr. Personality, but his efficiency and competence were the next best thing to automatic. The lieutenant certainly felt that way.

"Yeah," I said. "What's the matter with Rivetz? He seems a little out of it, today."

Martin grunted. "Not just today. All week. His wife's been diagnosed with cancer—she'd been ignoring a lump in her breast—and now she's supposed to have that surgery. It's really got him down," the lieutenant said.

"I'll bet."

"Hasn't affected his work yet, but you can only be depressed for so long before it starts to get to you. So I keep tabs. It makes me nervous he hasn't noticed yet that I've been doing it. When he does, he's going to kick me in the ass."

A television studio, when no taping is actually going on, is a remarkably noisy place, but not now. Everywhere we looked, plainclothes or uniformed cops had individuals or small groups aside, and were engaging them in earnest, but quiet confab.

Respect for the dead. In a couple of hours, the shock would be off, and all these TV people would return to being their usual brash selves. In fact, that night, out in L.A., after a number of facts about the case had leaked out, one West Coast talk show host sent a rival a full fried chicken dinner, along with a note that said, "My own personal recipe. Enjoy, sucka." This earned him a couple of rather unpleasant hours with the LAPD, doing a favor for their brother officers back East.

As for now, though, the jokes hadn't started, and the small gatherings of people huddled against the walls of the building and waiting to talk to someone in authority reminded me of nothing so much as Holy Saturday at St. Patrick's Cathedral. I had to admit, though, that if all *these* people were getting ready to make confessions, this case might never be solved.

We found Rivetz leading a team tossing Bentyne's dressing room.

The body was gone, but I've got to tell you something. If you've actually seen the stiff before it is taken away, the tape outline on the rug is no real help. Your memory and imagination team up to fill in that outline with a mental image that's even grislier than the reality. I had to blink away a mental image worthy of *The Exorcist* before joining reality.

The search was about done. Rivetz and the detectives had been neat, professional, and thorough—it looked as if the lieutenant had no need to worry about Rivetz's performance yet.

In fact, Rivetz seemed a lot more like his old self. The twisted smile was back on his seamed face. "Ah, Lieutenant," he said. "I was just about to send for you."

"Find anything?"

Rivetz took off his omnipresent Broderick Crawford Highway Patrol gray fedora, and ran his hand over the spikes of iron-gray hair that sprang up from his head, having not the slightest effect on them.

"Yeah, something," he said. "Let me catch you up before I show it to you, though. The ME agrees with me that it was probably arsenic that got him. They'll be doing a rush job on that—we gotta have a bone to throw the media types before they tear us poor civil servants to ribbons, right, Cobb?"

Gee, he was taunting me again, and everything. In a little while, he might forget he had a wife at all, let alone a sick one. "Right, Rivetz," I said.

"The other thing is, if the stuff was in the chicken, it may be no big help. Turns out everybody in the world knew he had this special fried chicken limoed in from Connecticut every day in an insulated picnic basket. So anybody who wanted to could make the opportunity to get to it."

He shrugged. "The next question, of course, is who wanted to, and we're working on that. Looks like a pretty long list, and what I found in here could make it longer."

Bentyne had a ceramic statue of Groucho Marx, about three feet high, in one corner of the dressing room. Rivetz went over to it and unscrewed the hand that held the cigar close to Groucho's mouth. Inside the hollow was a black velvet bag, the kind they sometimes put booze bottles in at Christmastime.

"I put it back after I let the lab guys take some to test. I didn't want to leave it lying around."

Rivetz brought the black bag to Bentyne's desk. I noticed that he stepped smack in the middle of the tape outline to get there. I always walk around. He opened the string on the bag and spilled the contents out onto the glass desktop. There were four little plastic bags, taped tight, each about the size and shape of an Italian sausage, and one a little smaller, maybe two thirds the size. Say a pound in all.

"There was an open one," Rivetz said. "I sent that off with the lab boys—don't worry they signed for it. I promised them the rest as soon as you saw it."

I asked permission, and fingered one of the bags. They contained a coarse, grayish-white powder. "Dope?" I said.

I was thinking, no wonder the shithead needed forty-five million dollars if this was his idea of a little stash. It was hard to figure, though. Bentyne was weird, but he didn't act like a junkie or even a cokehead.

Rivetz was shaking his head. "Beats the crap out of me," he said. "It's not like any dope I ever ran into, and I was on narcotics for six years. Didn't smell like it, didn't feel like it, so I ran a few street tests. It doesn't dissolve in water or alcohol—Bentyne has some aftershave in the bathroom over there—and it doesn't melt, it just chars and makes a smell like my Aunt Sophie used to make singeing the hair off her arms over the stove."

"Interesting," the lieutenant said. "Okay, send somebody to the lab with the rest—"

My phone rang. This was the new deal at the Network. No more beepers—cellular phones. I hated the goddam things. It's one thing to keep in touch; it's another to be constantly attached to your office by an electronic umbilical cord, even if it is invisible and runs through a satellite.

This time, though, I was glad I had it. I picked up and listened, then told the caller I was on my way and rang off.

"That was the Connecticut State Police," I said.

"Why'd they call *you?*" Rivetz demanded.

"Tell you on the way."

The lieutenant raised an eyebrow. "We're all going?"

"I think you'll want to. They just caught someone breaking into Bentyne's house."

"He's a *good* boy."
—MAE QUESTEL
Scott Towels commercial

9

She sat on a gurney in the emergency room of St. Mary's Hospital in Stamford, smiling at us and talking as if she were entertaining us in a living room.

"Thank you, gentlemen, for coming. I do so want to talk to someone. I'm so embarrassed, and I must look a fright."

She didn't look close to a fright. She wasn't as polished as she might ordinarily be—the bandage on her hand covered a good forty or fifty stitches from where she'd punched through the glass in Richard Bentyne's kitchen door, and there were a few consequent spots of blood on her frilly white silk blouse and her lavender suit. A few wisps of soft gray hair had escaped her chignon. She was pale, partly from shock, partly from loss of blood, and partly, no doubt, from painkillers.

She definitely looked as if she'd been through something, but she didn't look a fright. She looked like a bright
(blue) eyed, ever-so-slightly plump, wrinkle-free, attractive lady in her mid-fifties. Give her brown hair, and she
could have been the model for the Betty Crocker of my
youth.

She *definitely* did not look the obsessive nutcase who
had frustrated police forces across the country. But she
was.

Her name was Barbara Bentyne Anapole, and she was
originally from Akron, Ohio, an ordinary housewife and
mother until about eight years ago. We learned her sad
story from a Connecticut State Trooper who was more
than glad to surrender her to the NYPD because (1) a
murder case took precedence over a mere breaking and
entering, (2) because she was currently a legal resident of
New York, and (3) because Connecticut didn't have the
foggiest notion of what to do with her.

Nobody said so in so many words, but I got the impression that the guardians of the Nutmeg State would feel
less sadness about the passing of a rising American superstar than they otherwise might because his death probably
meant that they wouldn't have to go on busting this unbalanced, but otherwise nice old lady.

You couldn't even blame her for being unbalanced.
Eight years ago, she'd been home, fixing Thanksgiving
dinner while her husband drove around Akron in the
minivan, picking up their two sons and their families. The
vehicle was full of passengers and on its way home when
they were broadsided by a drunk driver, and driven into
oncoming traffic. The only survivor of the family had been
a daughter-in-law Barbara had never liked anyway.

Husband, kids, grandkids, boom, gone. One second,
family, next second, no family. I don't know if I could
face it.

Unfortunately, just about that time, a young comedian

named Richard Bentyne was coming to prominence. It so happened that as a teenager, Mrs. Anapole had had a son out of wedlock, whom she gave up for adoption. With the logic of desperation, out of the aching need not to be alone, she decided that Richard Bentyne was the long-ago departed infant. He had her maiden name, didn't he? He had blond hair and blue eyes like her family, didn't he?

She denied or ignored everything that didn't fit her desires. For instance, the fact that Richard Bentyne had a living set of parents all present and accounted for, or the fact that he was at least five years too old to be the child she'd put up for adoption.

When you tried to raise these facts, she'd just smile an indulgent, motherly smile and tell you that the press would say just anything these days, it was just a disgrace.

"There I was, just sitting in my apartment—" She lived in a high-rise across the street from Lincoln Center and went to the opera frequently. Insurance and her late husband's investments had left her well fixed. "Just sitting in my apartment," she said, "having a cup of coffee. I love a cup of fresh-brewed coffee in the middle of the morning, it perks me right up. In the afternoon, though, I like tea. Wouldn't you gentlemen like a cup of tea? Young man!"

She stopped an orderly and gave him a tea order. "And plenty of cream, sugar, and lemon, now," she concluded.

The orderly was about to be offended when Lieutenant Martin flashed him his shield and said, too quietly for the lady to hear, "Homicide investigation. Besides, I heard the doctor tell her to force fluids. Just do it, okay?"

The orderly thought it over for a few seconds, then said, "Uh, okay."

She smiled happily at us again. "Now, where was I?"

"Watching television and drinking coffee."

"That's right." She nodded at me like a second-grade teacher at a bright pupil. "Well, there I was, and they interrupted *Phil Donahue,* and came on with a news bulletin saying My Richard was dead.

"That was a very cruel thing to do, you know, even for the press. They might have known I'd be watching, or at least that I'd find out about what they'd said. Of course, I was shocked at first, but then I recognized it for the cruel joke it was."

"How?" I asked.

I saw that indulgent smile for the first time. "A mother knows," she said. "When the . . . tragedy . . . happened out in Akron, you know, I felt something at the moment it happened. I think I already knew when I saw the policeman coming up the walk.

"But let's not talk of unhappy things. Are you religious?" she asked.

"I'm not an atheist," I told her. It seemed to make her happy.

"Well, I firmly believe that the Lord doesn't try us beyond our strength. I lost many people I loved, but then I found Richard. Now, I know how busy and successful he is, and that he doesn't have a lot of spare time to spend with me, but I'm not one of those possessive mothers you read about. I understand he's a grown man, now, and needs to spread his wings and make his own decisions.

"Still, on a day like today, with the media telling such nasty lies about him— Can't you do anything about that, Mr. Martin?"

Lieutenant Martin looked as uncomfortable as I felt. "Um, no, ma'am. Unfortunately, the media gets to say pretty much what it wants to."

Especially, I thought, when it's the truth. Eventually, somebody was going to have to tell her that she'd lost her (delusionary) second family as well as her first. I was just glad it wasn't going to be me.

"It seems disgraceful they can get away with that. How-

ever, I decided that after dealing with something like that,
I would do something I'd never done before. I'd go to
Richard's house and let myself in and make him a good
home-cooked meal. It would be something comforting to
come home to."

"How did you know how to get there?"

"Oh, I've been there many times. Sometimes I just like
to take the train up from the city, get a taxi at the station,
and just sit in the car awhile and admire how far my boy
has come. Why, even the taxi drivers know him personally."

Which explained, I thought, how Barbara Anapole
found the place in the beginning—undoubtedly, Bentyne
had used taxis around here sometimes, and the drivers
had, understandably enough, remembered where the star
lived. I had no trouble believing Mrs. Anapole could have
convinced them that she was Richard Bentyne's mother; I
had to keep reminding myself it wasn't true.

"Today, when I came, I didn't just sit in the taxi and
look; I got out and paid him and sent him away. And then
I realized I'd forgotten my keys."

"Your keys," the lieutenant said.

"Yes," she said. She lowered her voice conspiratorially.
"Richard gave them to me after he first moved in here. At
one of our secret meetings. We have to have secret meetings because of That Woman." For the first time, Mrs.
Anapole didn't seem so nice.

"You mean Vivian Pike?"

She gave me a grim nod. "That's the one. She'll do
anything to keep my son and me apart. She wouldn't even
let my phone calls go through. And it's all so unnecessary.
I'm not one of those jealous or possessive mothers. I'm the
kind of mother who wants her son to find a nice girl."

I detected a little extra emphasis on the word "nice."

"I would be happy if he were married, though. Young

people today mock marriage, but in a marriage, you know where you stand."

"Did you make the chicken, Mrs. Anapole?"

She smiled brightly. "What chicken?"

"The chicken," I said, "that Mr. Gambrelli, the driver, drove into New York with for your—for Richard's lunch."

"Oh, I'm glad he'll have at least one good meal today. No, I didn't make any chicken. I never even got inside. I tried to force the door open, and the glass broke, and I cut my hand horribly. It was such a foolish thing to do, but I wanted to be there for my son."

"Yeah," the lieutenant said. "Will you excuse us for a moment, ma'am? We'll be right back."

"But we haven't had our tea!" she protested.

I'd forgotten all about it, but sure enough, at the moment, the orderly returned with a tray on which sat a pot of boiling water, some tea bags, some foam cups, sugar, lemon, and little plastic things of nondairy creamer. He smiled like a waiter, told us his name (Vernon), and even poured for us.

All I could figure was that he'd been hypnotized by the flashing of the lieutenant's tin, and was now convinced he was Nick Carter undercover on the trail of Dr. Quartz. Or maybe he knew that Mrs. Anapole would go for her purse and tip him two bucks, which she did, and he needed the money.

In any case, we had our tea now, and we stood there sipping it exactly as though we actually wanted it, while trading remarks about gardening. Rivetz, it turned out, grew roses in his garden out in Queens, and Mrs. Anapole had been a prize rose grower in her day. My eyes glazed over, but I fought to keep from showing it. As a Manhattanite, I feel the only place vegetable matter really needs to be is floating next to matzoh balls in a good chicken soup.

Finally, after I'd heard more about fertilizers and aphids than I ever cared to, we were done, and the lieutenant again made our excuses. She graciously granted us leave.

We withdrew to a little supply closet.

"Jesus," Lieutenant Martin said, "what are we going to do with her?"

"Bust her," Rivetz said, "She's a loon. She probably did it. Maybe she was aiming for the girlfriend."

"What's the matter," I said, "don't like the way she grows roses?"

"Her roses are fine. I just think when you have a homicide on one hand and a nut on the other hand, they just naturally go together." The seams in his face got smaller, tighter, and more numerous. "Besides, I know you're a TV expert and the lieutenant's known you since you were a baby, but that don't make you a cop, and never will. All right?"

"Take it easy, Rivetz," the lieutenant said.

"I'm taking it fine. I just don't need to be razzed by an amateur in the middle of a homicide investigation."

Fair is fair, and he was right. "I'm sorry, Rivetz. I didn't mean any disrespect."

His small dark eyes looked disappointed, as though he'd not only been expecting a fight, but wanting one, too.

Still, he nodded at me, and said, "Just so we know where we stand." A few seconds later, he added, "Hospitals. God, they make me depressed."

It was as close to a conciliatory gesture as he was ever likely to make.

"Is that all you have against her?" the lieutenant demanded. "Just a hunch?"

"Yeah," Rivetz said. "For now. What the hell, check into it, right? I mean, she could have a motive, easy. Maybe she's faced the fact that he's not her son, or that he'll never admit it. Or maybe it was aimed at the Pike woman, the one she saw coming between her and Bentyne."

"Means? If it's arsenic, the way we figure—"

The lieutenant shook his head. "I'm going to be glad when we get that lab report."

"I know what you mean," Rivetz said. "But look, if it is arsenic, well, you can get that anywhere. Rat poison, roach poison. When I was a kid, there used to be flypaper."

"There still is," I said. "I heard about some today."

"You did?" Rivetz said. "Where?"

"At the studio. Bates sent the producers of the show a bunch of stuff he uses, living out in the mountains like that. Kerosene lamp. Snowshoes. Flypaper, a few sheets of which disappeared, things like that. I think they were going to have a sort of show and tell on the air, with Bates being picturesque about what each thing is used for."

Mr. M stared at me. "Matty?" he said softly. "You suspected arsenic poisoning?"

"Right."

"And you knew they had this flypaper?"

"Uh huh."

"And it never occurred to you to tell me about it?" His voice was no longer soft.

I had to admit that in retrospect, it did seem rather dumb. I defended myself by pointing out that I was younger than Rivetz, and had never seen flypaper, at least the poisoned kind, actually in use. In fact, my only exposure to the stuff had been a Dashiell Hammett story.

"Call the studio on that gadget of yours. I want to tell them to find that stuff and latch hold of it, get some to the lab."

I did so. When Mr. M was done and had handed me back the phone, I said, "If it was the flypaper, that lets the mother off the hook."

Rivetz reminded me that she wasn't the mother.

"You know what I mean," I said. "Anyway, she's pretty clean on the opportunity issue, too. As far as I can make out the times from back at the studio and from the hospital log, Mrs. Anapole was having her hand sewn up here just about the same time the basket of chicken was showing up at the studio. I grant you it sat around for a while, and anybody there might have gotten to it, but it would have been awfully hard for her—she *wasn't* there."

Rivetz shook his head. "There's no problem there. I talked to the Pike woman. Somebody named Frances Jarmy comes on a daily basis to clean up and to make Bentyne's lunch—wouldn't you think a guy getting paid as much money as your Network was giving him could eat at a goddamn restaurant?"

"There were dietetic considerations," I said. "Go on."

"Yeah. Try and stop me. Anyway, Jarmy would make the lunch and hand it over to Gambrelli when he showed up. If Jarmy had to go out before Gambrelli showed up, the stuff was left on the front porch with a note. Tell me why Mother Machree over there couldn't have switched baskets."

"I think," I said, "that I would really treasure a talk with Frances Jarmy about now."

The lieutenant grunted. "Me, too. The state cops are looking. Local boys in the Weston area, too."

"In the meantime, I want to have a look at Bentyne's house," Rivetz said. "We're out of state—do we need a warrant?"

"No," I said.

"Don't tell me—you're a lawyer, too."

"No, but I am an officer of the Network. We own the house. A free house to live in was part of Bentyne's deal."

The lieutenant just grunted again, but Rivetz couldn't stand it. "Free houses. Multimillion-dollar salary. For what? For bullshitting on television. There's no justice at all in this goddamn world."

"Oh, I don't know," I said. "You're the one with the dangerous job, ducking bullets and all that, right?"

"Yeah?"

"But Bentyne is the one who's dead."

Rivetz pursed his lips. "Good point," he said.

"I want to get out there, too," the lieutenant said. "But what are we going to do with Mother Hubbard over there? Nobody in this state is willing to bust her or commit her, but I'm damned if I'm going to let her run around loose."

The answer was obvious to me, and had been for some time now, but *I* would be damned if I would be the one to say it, as touchy as everybody was lately.

There was silence for a long time. When Rivetz finally broke down and said, "I guess we have to take her with us," I suppressed a smile.

"Robin, I believe this calls
for a session with the Bat Cave's
computerized crime files."
—ADAM WEST
Batman, ABC

10

We cleared our visit with local authorities, who
after checking that I was representing the Network as legal
owner, grumbled a little and let us be.

We drove out in the lieutenant's unmarked car, him in
the front with Rivetz, me in the back with Mrs. Anapole.
She was awfully quiet as we traveled, and as I watched her,
the Demerol they'd given her at the hospital finally began
to click in. Her eyes would droop and her head would loll,
until she jerked herself awake with a wide-eyed snap of the
neck.

"Hang in there," I told her. "We'll be there before you
know it. Then you can lie down."

She squinted at me. "Do you think it will be all
right?" Her words were a little slurred. "I mean, do you

think Richard will mind?" Through the fog came genuine worry.

"No," I said truthfully. "I'm sure Richard won't mind."

In the front seat, Rivetz let out a low whistle, and I wanted to slug him.

"You know, Matty," the lieutenant said, "you may be representing the legal owner and all that, but you still don't have a key to this place, do you?"

"Don't need one," Rivetz growled. "We can get in where Moth—where the lady here broke the window."

"Precisely," I said smugly, exactly as though the matter had even crossed my mind.

And that's what we did. There was broken glass outside the door and a goodly amount of blood with it, but Rivetz crunched across, reached through the hole, and opened up. I was afraid our guest might be affected by the sight of a coagulating pool of her own personal gore, but by now, she was too woozy to notice.

I led her through to the living room, and put her down on the big leather couch with a couple of cushions.

"Want the afghan?" I asked.

"Yes," she buzzed. "Thank you, Richard."

I ignored it. I made sure she'd taken her shoes off, then I covered her. I took her injured right hand and placed it across her chest, just under her breast, so that it wouldn't fill with blood and swell while she was out. In a matter of seconds, she was snoring.

"Maybe she oughta adopt *you*," Rivetz said. "Now that there's a vacancy, I mean."

"Rivetz," I said, "I never met anybody like you. You can't even stand the *sight* of someone being decent to another human being."

"Fine. Sit here and be decent and baby-sit her while the lieutenant and I look around the house."

"Not necessary," I told him.

"No?" She could be faking, you know. As soon as you

leave the room, she could be up off that couch and out of here, and who knows who could wind up dead?"

"She's not going anywhere," I said. "Stay here a second. I'll be right back."

I dashed out to the kitchen, opened a wall panel, pushed a few buttons on a security console, and rejoined them.

"There," I said. "Now the whole place is alarmed except the door we came in by." I picked up Mrs. Anapole's shoes and slipped them into my pocket. "Now, if she wants to leave, it has to be barefoot over broken glass."

"Oh."

"Yeah. I said I was decent, not an idiot. There is a difference."

"Matty," the lieutenant said, "lighten up."

I didn't feel like lightening up. "I *know* she's a few pictures shy of a portfolio, all right? I just happen to sympathize with what made her that way."

I spread my hands. "Look, I'm a grown man, my father died last year of natural causes, and I still haven't completely gotten over it. This woman lost her whole family in a *second*. It might send me around the bend, if it happened to me. You, I suppose are immune."

Rivetz looked at me as if I were a slug he'd found in the lettuce on his Whopper. He stared at me for a long time.

"You think so?" he said. They were the three bitterest words I'd ever heard, and suddenly I remembered what the lieutenant had told me this morning.

I hastened to apologize, but Rivetz went on before I could get any of the words out.

"Listen, Cobb. My wife's name is Marie. I met her in junior high school. In high school we dated, then I went into the army. I traveled a lot, met a lot of girls. But it was a funny thing. Some of them reminded me of Marie, and the rest of them made me wish they did.

"When I got out, by some miracle she was still available, so I married her. For thirty years she's been a cop's wife. You know what being a cop's wife is, Cobb? Of course you don't, how could you? Being a cop's wife is the only job in the world tougher than being a cop.

"We're old-fashioned, Cobb. We live in a little house in Queens, and Marie keeps it clean and decent and cheerful, and when I go there, I can forget the shit we wade in in the streets. We weren't lucky enough to have kids, but we've been happy together.

"Only now she's going to die, Cobb. She's going to die. She doesn't have to, but she's going to. Because she won't have the operation she needs to live. Says she doesn't want to be 'mutilated.' Says it wouldn't be fair to me."

He gave a little bewildered laugh. "Can you believe that? Married to this woman for over thirty years, and she thinks I'm such a bastard that something like that is going to matter to me?"

He took off his hat and rubbed uselessly at his hair.

"I don't even know what to say to her," he went on. "We sit around the house with the TV on and pretend to watch it, and then I go to work and deal with death all day long, then I go home at night and deal with it some more."

He pointed at me. "So, Cobb, do me a favor. Don't tell me I'm immune from anything. I'm losing my whole family by inches only because she wants to die."

I told him I was sorry. It sounded, as it always does in circumstances like this, pitifully inadequate.

"Forget it," he said. "I'm sorry I mistook you for Ann Landers."

"You two done?" the lieutenant asked. He was trying to sound impatient, but I think he was glad Rivetz had let some of his troubles out. "Come on, we've got work to do."

This was the point at which Rivetz usually reminded me that the *cops* had work to do, and that I was merely along for the ride, but apparently, we had entered an Era of Good Feeling, of which I heartily approved. I didn't risk upsetting it by taking part in the search, a chore that is too much like housework to appeal to me, anyway.

Instead, I followed them around, a polite little representative of the owner, giving them permission to do anything they felt would solve the case, occasionally going back to check our elderly Sleeping Beauty.

Whatever they felt, the case didn't get solved.

The house was surprisingly empty. For somebody who faced the prospect of having forty-five million dollars to spend furnishing his (free) domicile over the next several years, Richard Bentyne, to judge by his house, had come down with a surprising case of galloping frugality.

There was none of the stuff that marks a house as your own—quirky furniture, artwork, knickknacks, souvenirs, anything. There wasn't much in the way of clothes, and there was *no* mess at all. Even his toothbrush bristles were neat and square.

It was as if he used up so much of his personality on the air, he didn't have enough left to impose on his house, even after having lived there for over six months.

It was kind of sad. This was turning into National Understand a Pathetic Wretch Day. By the end of it, I'd be one myself.

Of course, as Rivetz pointed out, if you were a devotee of white powders, such as had been found in his dressing room, you'd have reason to husband even a large income.

We did find various white powders in the house—sugar and cornstarch in the kitchen. His bath powder was green, and the laundry detergent in the pantry was blue. There was none of the strange, coarse stuff that we'd seen earlier in the day.

The only room that showed any promise at all was a small den/office off the living room. There was an IBM PC there, and a box of floppies next to it.

Lieutenant Martin read off labels.

"Skit ideas. Poss stunts, solo. Poss stunts, with guests. Monologue topix. Jarmy. Odd news stories—"

"Jarmy?" I said.

"Yeah. Oh, right. That's the name of the housekeeper."

"The chicken chef. I'd like to know what's on that." Rivetz said.

"Have to bring it into headquarters and get one of the wizards to go through all this stuff and tell us what's on it."

"Good idea," I said. "But I hate to wait for the Jarmy disk."

"Yeah. So what are we supposed to do? You know how to run these things?"

"In a limited way," I said. "I couldn't break into the Pentagon for you, but I can read a damn disk."

"Fine. I hereby deputize you to do it."

"Okay, move," I said.

I sat at the console and booted up. Then I put the Jarmy disk in, and called for the directory.

I had a heavy breathing cop over each shoulder.

"Don't you need a password or something?" Rivetz said.

"Apparently not," I said, as the directory blinked on. "After all, he was the only one who used this machine, what's he got to hide?"

"Well, he was cheating on his live-in girlfriend, and he was stashing some weird shit in his dressing room, you know?"

I had a list of files to call up. There weren't any, unfortunately, entitled POISONED CHICKEN, or any that mentioned chicken at all. I passed up BEDMAKING, DUSTING, and EMPLOYMENT CONDITIONS, among others, and went for D. ROUT.

"Let's try this one," I said.

"What the hell," agreed my companions.

And that was the one. It started with a message in flashing caps: **DO NOT ARRIVE BEFORE MR. BENTYNE'S DEPARTURE AT 9:15 A.M.**

"Immediately upon arrival," it went on, "you will prepare Mr. Bentyne's lunch of oven-fried chicken prepared to the following recipe. Note: **YOU MUST NOT DEPART FROM THIS RECIPE.**"

I read the recipe. "Well, that settles that, " I said.

"What settles what?" the lieutenant wanted to know.

"The fried chicken. Bentyne went into such a snit about his gluten allergy, he couldn't have wheat in any form, you remember I told you about that. Then, I hear he has fried chicken zoomed in from his personal kitchen every day for lunch. See, here it is, 'Place chicken in insulated container and give it to driver from Network.' "

I shook my head. "This guy must have been a Hugh Hefner fan. Anyway, I never heard of fried chicken made without flour, have you?"

Mr. M said, "I ought to refuse to answer any questions about fried chicken on the grounds of political correctness, but no, I haven't."

"Neither have I," I said. "Until now. This recipe calls for finely crushed potato chip crumbs with cheese and garlic for the breading." I thought about it. "Sounds pretty good."

"Garlic," Rivetz said. "Perfect. Arsenic has a garlicky taste."

"Yeah," the lieutenant said, "but—"

I never did find out what his objection was, because at that second, an eardrum-busting scream tore the air between us and the living room.

She woke up, I thought stupidly, and headed for our guest.

It hadn't been a dream she was screaming at. A large black man with dreadlocks a foot and a half long stood in the doorway. A broken brown paper bag was at his feet, and various grocery items were plopping or rolling (as their shapes dictated) on the floor.

I saw him; he saw me; he ran; I chased.

Sort of. I'd taken about three steps across the carpet when I stepped on a stick of butter or something, and lost my balance.

This set me staggering, which would have been all right—I've fallen down before—except my momentum was taking me right to the open back door and an appointment to be sliced up like corned beef at $6.98 a pound on the broken glass out on the deck.

I didn't know what to do, so I just tried to keep moving. It worked. My greasy soles somehow skated across the glass as if it were rough ice, and then I had the edge of the deck to worry about.

I went off it like a crippled duck, and this time I did fall, hard, on the gravel walk. I struggled to my feet (not the easiest thing in the world to do on gravel, by the way) and resumed the chase.

It wasn't long before I could see it was hopeless. He was too far ahead of me; in a few seconds, he'd be out of the wooded area around the house, and out on the road, where he undoubtedly had a car stashed.

Time to try a wild one. "Stop or I'll shoot!" I yelled.

He didn't stop. But he did look back over his shoulder. This caused him to veer from the center of the path, which in turn caused his head to make the sudden and intimate acquaintance of a fat, droopy willow branch.

He was easy to catch up with now, mainly because he was stretched full length out on the gravel.

As Rivetz never tires of pointing out, I am not a cop, and I demonstrated to myself once again that it's much better that way.

I was about three steps away from my quarry, just getting ready to dive on him and finish him off, when two heavy hands grabbed me by the shoulders and damn near pulled me off my feet.

"Easy, Tarzan," the lieutenant said. "You'll get yourself in a whole lot of trouble."

"But he—but he—"

"But he *what?*" the lieutenant demanded, then answered his own question. "He walked through an unlocked door; a woman saw him, and screamed."

"But—"

"He didn't hurt anybody, he didn't take anything. All he did was run when three big guys started chasing him."

The lieutenant took a deep breath. "Getting too old for all this running," he said. "Look, Matty, if it had been a blond white man in a gray business suit that walked in, what's her name would never have screamed, and you wouldn't have been so convinced you were chasing a killer."

He dropped his voice. "The real shame of it is, neither would I."

I was pissed off. My knees hurt where I'd skinned them on the gravel, but that was the least of it. What really bothered me was the fact that Mr. M was right.

"Well, what the hell was he *doing* here, then?"

"Maybe he came to read the meter," Rivetz suggested.

"Why don't you ask him?" the lieutenant said.

I said, "Huh?" Then I looked down and saw he was right. Our guest had been dazed, but apparently not knocked out. Right now, he was lying there, taking it all in. I asked him how he was.

"Why you want to skeer me like dat, mon?"

"I jumped to a conclusion."

He grinned. "So I 'eer. Don't let it trouble you, mon. If I see the brudder 'ere come for me, I might be just as quick to run."

I'm not going to transcribe the sound of him any more. Suffice it to say he had a full-fledged Jamaican accent.

He declared that his head hurt, but that he was okay. Rivetz didn't stand still for it. He pulled a little flashlight out of his pocket and checked the guy's pupils, then made the man follow his finger.

"You seem all right," Rivetz admitted grudgingly. "You should see a doctor."

"Later, later, man. Maybe first, you like to tell me what you are doing in Mr. Bentyne's house?"

"Ah," I said. I got my card out of my wallet. "I am Matt Cobb, I work for the Network, which owns this house, and I'm helping Lieutenant Martin and Detective Rivetz investigate it."

They showed him their buzzers.

He read them carefully. "City of New York. What are you doing here, then? What's going on?"

The lieutenant said, "Routine investigation," and he and Rivetz went immediately into Serious Cop Mode. "Would you mind telling us who you are?"

"Jarmy," he said. "Francis Jarmy. I do cooking and cleaning for Mr. Bentyne."

Oh, great, I thought. Another wrong assumption.

They asked him questions, and he answered them. They didn't have to read him his rights yet, because this was a field investigation.

He'd worked for Bentyne for six months, since the comedian had come East. He had a whole bunch of clients, but Bentyne paid the best because he was so particular about the way things were done. Jarmy flew back to Jamaica about once or twice a month. He got along with Bentyne fine, considering he'd only laid eyes on the man one time, when he'd been hired. Ditto Vivian Pike. He didn't know of any enemies Mr. Bentyne might have had. Why, had something happened to Mr. Bentyne?

The cops ignored him, and kept on asking questions.

Jarmy used to consult the computer recipe every day, but now he had it perfectly memorized and seldom bothered. If there were ever special instructions, a disk would be left out marked for his notice; otherwise he followed the routine.

Had he made the chicken today?

"Of course I did, mon. What's the matter, didn't he like it?"

"Well," I said. "He ate it. Listen, when you were cleaning up, did you ever find any drugs around the house?"

"No way. He told *me* no drugs. He hated them. If he used them, I wouldn't have worked for him. It's hard enough for a Rastaman to have a business dealing with white folks without drugs coming into it. Ganja is holy, but I only smoke it when I go home."

On that joyful note, the lieutenant decided to move things inside. Mrs. Anapole was fully awake now. When she saw Jarmy she said, "Oh, Francis, how nice to see you. However did you hurt your head?"

Turned out they were old friends—Jarmy would be coming or going during the times Barbara had the driveway staked out.

I shook my head. This was getting too weird. I wished I could just go home and walk the dog.

"You know he really *is*
Man's Best Friend."
—BILL BURRUD
Kal Kan commercial

11

It was a couple of hours before I got my wish, and
the sun had a late-afternoon red tinge to it when I got
back to the city and retrieved Spot from the apartment
two floors below mine, where he had been spending the
weekend with Max and Sara Bialosky, and their English
nanny, Miss Featherstone, pronounced "Fearson," don't
ask me.

The kids scratched Spot behind his ears, and kissed him
good-bye. It isn't smart to kiss a Samoyed, especially in
the summertime. Little Max and Sara would undoubtedly
be picking dog hairs out their mouths until bedtime.

Spot wasn't actually my dog, but I owed him a lot, my
life on several occasions. I owed him something of even
more importance to a New Yorker, especially a Manhattanite. I owed him my apartment.

Well, not my apartment. His.

Spot's owners were college friends of mine, Rick and Jane Sloan, the couple Born Out of Time.

I say that, because they were handsome and rich and clever and eccentric in a way that was much more than the rich version of nuts. They were like refugee rich folks from a 1930s musical.

The name, for instance. As I mentioned, Spot is a Samoyed, a medium-size Siberian dog bred to pull sleds. He has bright black eyes, perpetually smiling black lips, a black home-plate shape for a nose, pointy little ears, and a big cloud of pure white fur, each hair of which sticks straight out from his body.

So Rick named him Spot.

When I asked what for, he said, "My God, Matt, he's named for the gigantic white spot that covers his entire body."

Eccentric. But I have to admit, their eccentricity did lead them to find a use for their money other than buying ever more expensive electronic toys from The Sharper Image.

They went to a lecture at the Museum of Natural History, and got bit by the archaeology bug. I mean, they got it *bad*. Not only did they decide to sponsor an expedition, they went along on it. Since they'd both majored in Nothing Much in college (Rick, at six eight was my teammate on the basketball team), they went along as simple grunt labor.

This involved them in things they'd never experienced before. Sweating somewhere other than at the tennis club. Getting actual dirt on their actual hands. Growing calluses.

It was a revelation to them, and they kept finding (and working on) new digs.

What this meant to me was that what had started out as a six-month doggie-and-apartment-sitting gig for a couple of friends had stretched out over years, and I was getting spoiled. I had come to think of the Central Park West penthouse as home. I subscribed to magazines from there. It was my voting address. I had now had possession of Spot longer than they had had, even if I didn't pay for his obedience and attack training, or for his silver-studded collars. I did buy him special pet-store-only dog food and used this smelly blue shampoo on him that kept him extra fluffy and white, but I figured that was the least I could do.

In the meantime, I lived in constant fear for the Sloans. Archaeology, at least the Sloans' kind, seems to happen only in dangerous places. I don't know why ancient civilizations left their ruins in war-torn hell holes like the Middle East or Indochina rather than St. Louis Park, Minnesota, or Montclair, New Jersey, but they did.

So the Sloans went to the Middle East, and Indochina, and risked bugs and sun, and dug. Not only that, but it wasn't safe to be an American in a lot of those places. It was even less safe to be a *rich* American.

I worried about them not only because I liked them a lot but because if they were killed, *somebody* would inherit this apartment, and the odds were extremely slim that it would be me. It would probably be somebody like cousin Beauregard Sloan, of the Tidewater Sloans, or something like that.

But there was no need to borrow trouble. I had enough of that already.

On the way out of the building, I asked Ramiro, the doorman, if he was done with his *New York Times*. He looked at Spot, smiled, and handed it over. The traffic was light, pre–rush hour, so we jaywalked across the street to the park.

Once there, I kept Spot on the lead until he had attended to his alimentary requirements, then told him sternly to wait while I pulled out a page.

I deposited the parcel in a wastebasket (I've always

wondered how guys who empty those things feel about the pooper-scooper law), found a bench, and let Spot run free for a while.

He looked at me when I did it. This was a rare treat, and he was making sure it wasn't some mistake.

I patted his head. "Go," I said. "Enjoy."

So he went. He got involved in a Frisbee game with a couple of teenagers. He made a very pretty tableau—the white dog against the green grass, silver buildings, the blue sky, with the red disk in his mouth and the laughing kids around him; it was one of those New York Moments, the kind where, if you love the place, you can forget the strife and the crime and the pollution and the incompetence and just revel in it. There are a lot fewer of those these days than there used to be. Or maybe I was just getting old.

In any case, I enjoyed it, and it had the added benefit of taking my mind off Richard Bentyne and his murder for thirty whole seconds.

But my mind was back on it, now, so I thought about it.

It didn't do any good to say it was a mess. That was the kind of information you could get from an accountant— 100 percent accurate and absolutely useless. To do myself any good, I'd have to work out exactly what kind of mess it was.

Well, to start off, it was a public relations nightmare. We pay the guy the earth to come to the Network, and he gets murdered on the job. Under the nose of a bodyguard.

This wasn't going to be so hot for morale, either.

Or for me. One of the reasons I was sitting here on a park bench rather than acting responsibly and manning my battle station at the Tower of Babble was the virtual certainty that Falzet was waiting there to tear off a wide strip of my hide.

That said, the heartless logic of the situation (and broadcasting knows no other kind) led to the conclusion that in the long run, this situation need not be so bad for the Network. No matter how many times Network executives had talked about building an audience for the new Bentyne show over time, that they didn't expect him to show up and walk on water and jump right to the top of the profitable fringe-time ratings, that was a lot of bull.

For forty-five million dollars, that was *exactly* what they expected. For that kind of money, they wanted him to walk on water, dominate the ratings, cure cancer, and talk Madonna into entering a Benedictine convent—on the air.

And he hadn't done it. He'd been building an audience—slowly. And this is not a patient business.

Maybe I should tell Lieutenant Martin to arrest Tom Falzet.

Seriously, though, no contract in show business is unbreakable. If they'd really gotten sick of Bentyne, they would have bought him out. Falzet himself had told me there was such a clause in the contract.

On a personal level, I knew from experience that Bentyne was a neurotic (to say the least) pain in the ass. And while it's not unheard of for people to get killed for being pains in the ass, that sort of thing usually happens on the spur of the moment, with a bottle of Schlitz across the temple in a bar or at a family cookout.

They *don't* happen as the result of mysterious poisonings.

Besides which, while Bentyne may have been a pain in the ass to everyone who knew him, he was also the meal ticket for virtually everybody involved. As far as I could tell, everyone involved in that show, except for the Network union-enrolled contract technical personnel, was out of a job as of now. And any of the union people who hadn't liked working with Bentyne could have asked for, and gotten, transferred.

You don't kill the source of your income, the goose that

lays the golden checks, just because he's a pain in the ass. You only do it if he's a mortal threat to you, if he's threatened to cut off the flow of gold or something worse.

This went even for the person with the most obvious motive—Vivian Pike. Of course, I only knew her extremely superficially, but she didn't give the impression of being so desperately in love with Bentyne that she'd kill him to keep him out of the arms of another woman.

Of course, if she'd poisoned the chicken, and was counting on her lover to bite the dust within the next half-hour or so, she might have created the impression of indifference just for me. She was the one, after all, who'd told me that Bentyne was having it off with Marcie, a fact, I suddenly realized in support of which I had only Vivian Pike's word.

Well, Lieutenant Martin's minions had been questioning everyone connected with the Bentyne show all day— they'd turn up anything that was there to be turned up along those lines.

Even if it were all true, though, it still didn't make sense. If this Vivian-Pike-of-the-mind, this jealous killer I'd been hypothesizing, were going to start offing people, the one to start with would have been Marcie.

It made psycho-political sense, in light of today's psycho politics. Vivian Pike was the producer of an important Network series because she was the star's girlfriend. Very un-PC. What she had to do was prove herself capable of the job as quickly as possible, and remove the bimbo-stigma. Even if she had gotten sick of Bentyne on a personal level, she had to know without him there was no job, and therefore no proof, and therefore no continued big-time.

So she wouldn't kill him for running around on her. From her point of view, guys to sleep with had to be easier to come by than top-quality jobs.

It might have been different if Bentyne had been pre-
paring to kiss her off as producer as well as two-time her
as lover, but that simply wasn't true. Just a couple of days
ago he had informed the Network that he was exercising
his contractual right to lock in Vivian Pike as his producer
for the next five years.

This left us with the unknown, what Lieutenant Martin
likes to call the Nut Factor.

Well, we certainly had nuts. Always did, since this
wasn't the kind of business that called forth sanity.

So who was there?

Alf Kriecz, the comedy writer and put-on artist? Didn't
know enough about him to be definitive, but all the things
I said about motive applied to him. There are a lot more
comedy writers than there are shows to write for.

Marcie Nast, the associate producer with the victim
mentality? The reverse of Vivian Pike. If she'd had somebody she wanted dead, it would have been the official
girlfriend and head producer. If Vivian had been on the
level, Marcie had nothing to fear from Bentyne. Literally
and figuratively, she had him by the balls. If he got tired
of playing footsie before she did, she could go the press
with a tale of sexual harassment, cry a little, and sue him
and the Network for a big hunk of that forty-five million.
Wouldn't matter if she won or not—the bad publicity
would be revenge enough.

Not loony enough? Okay let's go further out. Barbara
Bentyne Anapole. Sure, she might get violent if somehow
the reality about her "son" was ever brought home to her.
But how had she gotten at the chicken? Jarmy swore it was
never out of his sight until he handed it to Gambrelli, and
I knew for a fact that she hadn't been anywhere around
the studio that morning.

Not good enough? Okay, let's go really far out, as far out
as Montana. Clement Bates loomed large in the last week-

end plus of Richard Bentyne's life, though come to think about it, I didn't believe they ever had managed to come face to face.

Was Bates that nuts? Sure he was. I'm a strong believer in live and let live, but I'm sorry. Sane people do not turn their backs on hundred-million-dollar fortunes and go live like hermits.

But I had to face it—the very form of his nutsiness let him off the hook in my estimation. Even though he could have pranced unnoticed throughout the studio and poisoned everybody, what the hell was the *motive?* Delayed revenge on Bentyne for eating too much of Clem's bear meat and pemmican or whatever the hell Bates sustained himself on? Bates was the only person involved who was actually richer than Bentyne himself.

Then I thought of suicide. Not for myself. I mean that I thought of the possibility that Bentyne had committed suicide. It was a little hard to credit that somebody planning suicide would, in the first place, use arsenic, which is very nasty, when there are so many quicker and less painful poisons around, and in the second place, use the arsenic to dose up a batch of chicken, then sit there and munch away at, oh, judging by the bones I saw, two and a half pieces of it until he started to feel the effects.

I'd have to watch somebody doing that before I'd believe it.

So there I was. Nobody had killed Bentyne. He was fine; all this was just the biggest put-on of all.

I sighed, and watched Spot chasing the Frisbee. I noticed that wherever he was when he caught it, he always brought it back to the girl.

There was a chirp in my pocket. The cellular phone. I had forgotten to ditch it back at the apartment the way I'd intended to.

I took it out of my pocket and looked at it just as it chirped again. I was sorely tempted to chuck the thing into the pond and drown it, but duty overcame all, and I answered it.

"Cobb, this is Rivetz."

"How'd you get this number?"

"I'm a cop. I asked your office. They want you to check in."

"I'll bet they do. What's up?"

"I don't know if I ought to tell you. People can eavesdrop on these things."

"Not this one, it's one of the new digital systems."

"Like that's supposed to mean something, right? Anyhow we heard from the lab."

"Yeah?"

"We're all great detectives. Arsenic. Not from flypaper. Specifically a commercial preparation called Deth-on-Ratz, with a d-e-t-h and an r-a-t-z. Obtainable anywhere in the country. Untraceable. Not that we expected anything better. But the kicker is the white powder."

"What was it? Not a drug, right?"

"Depends what you mean. What it was, was powdered rhino horn. Can you imagine? I thought that was for old guys in Hong Kong."

"Rhino horn," I said.

"Yep. The lieutenant wants you to let him know if you think of anything."

"Sure," I said. But I was already thinking about things. Plenty of them. I called Spot. He barked and ran happily to me.

"Let's get moving," I told him.

"This is the old redhead,
out chere at the big ballpark."
—RED BARBER
New York Yankee Baseball, WPIX-TV, New York

12

Three and a half hours later, I was back in Central Park, about twenty blocks to the north, on one knee in the dirt with a metal mask on my face, looking past the hairless armpit of a guy named Wolf.

It had been a busy few hours. First, I'd gone back to the office to take my medicine with Falzet. He wasn't pleased with the murder, but he went ballistic when I told him about the rhino horn.

"That bastard!" he shouted. "That son of a bitch!"

That was unprecedented. Tom Falzet could buzz like a hornet when he got angry, or get hissy like a snake, but he never shouted and never swore.

"By Christ" (he never took the Name of the Lord in vain, either), "if he wasn't already dead I'd kill him myself."

He began to line out exactly why he was so upset, but I'd already been there ahead of him. This was the ultimate public relations nightmare.

Richard Bentyne was sleeping around? The public would shrug it off. That's what those show-biz types *do*, isn't it, Martha? Taking drugs? Tsk, tsk, an addictive personality. A couple of weeks at the Betty Ford Clinic is what he needs, and right away.

But *powdered rhino horn?* Taken from the recently butchered carcass of an endangered species? Not only was it disgusting (which it was, no argument there), but it was also *ungreen*.

I have probably said at some point in this story that Bentyne made fun of everything people had strong principles and beliefs about. If I did, I was wrong. He never joked about the two holy causes—AIDS or the environment.

These causes were *hip* as well as worthy. Half of Bentyne's audience probably mocked fur-coat wearers on the street. The rest had "Save the Whales" stickers on their cars.

But now, to find out he was using this . . . *stuff* would not only make him (with the Network as accessory) a dispoiler of the wild, it would also make this genius of mockery, this high priest of *hip*, out to be just as gullible an asshole as the old men in the East who took the stuff convinced it would help them keep their virility. Worse. A thousand years or more of their culture tell them their belief is true. Bentyne's culture made him nothing but a pathetic idiot.

"Is there any way we could keep this quiet?" Falzet demanded."

I coughed. "Excuse me, sir," I said. "I'm trying not to laugh in your face."

"Why not? They're your friends, aren't they?"

"Lieutenant Martin is a second father to me."

"Well?"

"Mr. Falzet, if I were Lieutenant Martin's only begotten son of flesh and blood, if I were his *clone*, he wouldn't sit on this story for me."

"Surely, there must be some way to persuade him."

"Sir, if you're talking about bribes or favors, here, I'm walking out."

"Don't be foolish," he hissed. "Bribes or favors. What do you take me for, Cobb?"

I let the question pass. Instead I said, "Look at it from the cops' point of view. What is the cops' biggest obstacle in a case like this?"

"I dislike guessing games."

"Then I'll just tell you. It's *us*."

"Us?"

"Yeah. Us. The Network. The media in general. Publicity and pressure."

He got very stiff. "Our stations are licensed to operate in the public interest, convenience, and necessity. We have our job to do."

"Of course we do, and I'm all for it. But we're looking at this from their point of view. Their job is to find out what scurries out when they lift the rocks. That can be difficult with a spotlight over your shoulder.

"And remember, they're only human. Nobody wants to wake up in the morning to read in the newspaper what an idiot he must be. 'If the murder of a prominent and influential citizen such as this remains unsolved, how much less secure must the average person feel,' and bla and bla and bla."

"What does this have to do with powdered rhinoceros horn?"

"It's a diversion. A gift from God, the way they see it. Now, instead of 'Why don't the police do something?' the media will be full of Bentyne and what a hypocritical sleazeball he was, and how stupid we were to have paid him forty-five million bucks with which he could subsidize the destruction of this magnificent beast, the gentle giant of the veldt, or wherever the hell it lives, who eats plants and only charges when attacked, and the rest of the *National Geographic Specials* spiel."

Falzet had his hand up. "Stop. Please stop."

"You get the idea."

Of course, all this speculation was based on the totally unproven and possibly baseless assumption that the rhino horn was actually Bentyne's, that it wasn't planted there by somebody else. After all, if somebody could get at Bentyne's chicken to poison it, they could get to his Groucho cookie jar, too. Might have done it at any time since they'd moved into the theater.

I didn't mention it, because it didn't matter. Falzet hadn't thought of it, and neither would ninety-nine and a big fraction percent of the public. When it comes to celebrity scandals, nobody's in the mood to let facts stand in the way of the fun.

"I have always," he said, "*had* the idea. I only wondered whether our stockholders and viewers could be prevented from getting the same idea. Apparently not."

"No, sir. It's like throwing the baby to the wolves," I said, although *National Geographic* would probably have corrections to make on that one, too.

"Precisely," Falzet said. Now that we had put it in terms of babies and wolves, we had reached a level he could understand, and even approve. I said he was an honest businessman. I never said he was a gentle one.

"Actually, considering the stink that's going to attach itself to Bentyne, probably the best thing for us to do, from the publicity angle, is put it out we killed him ourselves."

"Do you find this situation funny, Cobb?"

"No, sir. It's bravado. I always laugh in the face of catastrophe."

For a few seconds, I thought he was going to throw a paperweight at me, and so did he. He grabbed it, an abstract sculpture in jade, and gripped it so hard, his fingers turned white. His lips were white, too, from being pressed tight together. It was as if he didn't want to let the words out, as if what was in his mind to call me would scorch his mouth.

When he finally said anything, his voice was a whisper.

"Get out!" he said.

"Yes, sir. Actually, what you said before about them doing us a favor, I think they've already done us one."

He was bitter. "From their point of view, of course."

"Naturally. But it's something. I checked back with them just before I came in here, and Lieutenant Martin told me they'd break the story in a press release tomorrow morning at eleven."

"So?"

"So he didn't make me promise to keep quiet about it. I can go down and have a word or two in the newsroom, and they can break the story at eleven. Then we can be the first ones to kick Bentyne's corpse, as it were. Take some of the curse off our financing—indirectly—the obliteration of the rhino."

"And that, I suppose, is the best we're going to do."

"You could help it along with a statement disassociating the Network from anti-environmental practices etcetera, etcetera. The line about your killing Bentyne if he were still alive is possibly a bit much."

"I've already talked to Public Relations. I'll get them back in here."

I could tell from the expression on his face that he would have liked to have killed me, but I had brought Spot along for protection. Falzet had a lot of respect for Spot. I had had him growl at the man once.

"Cobb," he said, "fix this."

I was tempted to tell Spot to eat him. What did he expect me to do?

"Yes, sir," I said, "I'll hop the next plane to Africa and personally save a rhino from a poacher, after which I'll paint the Network logo on his hide so the world will know he's under our protection."

Falzet closed his eyes. "More bravado, I suppose."

"Yes, sir. With a leavening of pique. We can do a lot of things at Special Projects, but we can't unring a bell or uncrack an egg."

"You have imagination. Think of something. Create a diversion. Do what the police did—get the media interested in something other than the Network. We're not too far from the launch of the fall season, and beyond that lies the November sweeps. Something has to be done!"

And there you have it, I thought, Tom Falzet's saving grace as a businessman and as a human being. He really cared about the Network and about the work he did, and tried to do it as well and as nobly as a crabbed little soul could.

"Well," I suggested, "how about if I find the killer? Would that be okay?"

He thought it over. Seriously. The man was unkiddable; I don't know why I kept trying. Something about him made it irresistible. It occurred to me that I had fallen into the habit of treating Falzet the way Bentyne and Alf Kriecz and the rest of them treated the world. I resolved to stop.

Finally, Falzet said, "That would do it, if you can find the killer soon enough. Be as quick as you can."

It was apparent he wasn't going to make stopping easy. Still, I was a hero, and told him I'd get on it right away, and left.

My next two stops were still in the Tower of Babble, but many floors below. I went down to local news on the sixth floor and stayed awhile to have my brain picked. Then I told them that Lieutenant Martin and Mr. Falzet would both probably have statements for them.

Then it was back to the elevators and up two floors to the videotape library. All vertical movement in NetHQ is done via the stainless-steel elevators. If there were horizontal ones, we'd use them, too. God help us if there's ever a fire. I'm sure a good half the employees don't even know where the fire stairs are.

Bill Bevacqua, does though, because Bill knows everything. Bill is Network News's chief videotape librarian, and sees it all—what we put on the air, what we don't put on the air, stuff we've shot but wouldn't dare put on the air—everything.

Not only watches it but studies it, classifies it, and enters it into the computer retrieval system under as many headings as he thinks will be necessary.

You'd think a guy who spent his life in a windowless room doing this stuff would be a leech-white, one-eyed hunchbacked gnome, but Bill is ruddy-faced, slight but sturdy and straight, with a twinkle in the blue eyes behind the glasses. I must admit his hair is prematurely white, but he's still one of the healthier-looking off-the-air specimens we have around the place, especially in the technical department.

"Got a minute, Bill?" I asked.

"No. Come in. Good to see you, Matthew, even if I am busier than a one-armed paperhanger with piles. I bet I know why you're here."

"I bet you don't."

"You don't want to see the beautiful obit we're going to run on Richard Bentyne on the six-thirty feed of the *Evening News?*"

"What did you do, chroma-key in a halo?"

"You're casting aspersions on our journalistic objectivity again. We didn't make him all that saintly. Besides, all

I did was pull up the bits and pieces of tape. Assistant producer put the thing together. Can I help it if she was a big fan?"

"Made him look real good?"

"Pretty good. After all, he was our boy. Wasn't he?"

"Nope. He was a viper infiltrating our bosom. The assistant producer and whoever voiced it are going to be down here begging you to accidentally erase that tape."

"So this tape is an embarrassment. But that's not the one you want to see."

"Right."

"Well, what do you want to see?"

"Rhinos."

"Rhinos? As in rhinoceri?"

"I think it's rhinoceroses, actually."

"Never mind that. Big ugly animals with horns on their faces, and they live in Africa?"

"Well, beauty is in the eye of the beholder, but yeah, that's what I want. Don't you have it?"

"I have everything. I'm just trying to think of some connection."

"I'll give you a hint. I predict local news will be calling you very soon, asking for this very same stuff."

"That's no help," he said.

"All will become clear," I promised, "but not from me. Not only do I lack sufficient time to tell you, but going over it all again would depress the hell out of me."

"Oh, all right, be mysterious, if you have to." He punched a few buttons on his computer console, went back into a shelf, and came back with a big blue plastic tape-reel container.

"Next year we switch to disk," he said. "It'll increase our capacity tenfold." Then he found me an editing carrel and a technician to run the machines for me so I wouldn't get in trouble with the union.

Then I sat down and watched it. Not all of it. Would

you imagine the Network had accumulated like *three hours* of news footage on rhinos? Me neither, until I watched the first forty minutes of it or so and learned more about rhinos than I ever wanted to know.

I felt like the guy in the Ogden Nash poem, who ends up by wanting to look at something less "prepoceros." I thanked the techy, waved a thanks to Bill, and left.

As I was walking out the door, I heard his phone chirp. I listened for a few seconds as Bill said, "What? Yeah, I've got them. Yeah, right here in my hand." He put the tape down, placed the hand in question over the mouthpiece, and said to me, "You are a witch."

I laughed and walked out.

Now that I was fully armed with information, I had nobody to use it on. Naturally, *The Richard Bentyne Show* had not taped that evening, and when the cops were done, people went their own ways. Vivian Pike, my sources told, was in seclusion with a friend who "lived someplace in the Village."

There are five boroughs in New York City, and Greenwich Village is only a small part of one of them, but its narrow, convoluted streets seem to hide more someplaces than the rest of the city combined, so I'd save her until tomorrow.

That left Marcie Nast among the Network people, who, I learned, spent every summer Monday night playing softball in a mixed league in Central Park. Central Park is even harder to find people in than the Village, assuming she wasn't in seclusion mourning Bentyne's death somewhere.

I knew where Barbara Anapole was, but I didn't think I could learn much more from her, and I didn't really want to see what state her delusions had gotten to by now, anyway. Francis Yarmy was undoubtedly up in Stamford, maybe calling people on his waiting list to inform them that now he had a hole in his schedule, and would they like to fill it.

Clement Bates, whom no one knew what the hell to do with, was staying at Network expense at the New York Hilton, just down the road a little and across the street from Network Headquarters. It tells you all you need to know about my state of mind to say that I was considering dropping in on him.

The thing was, even without Falzet's request for a miracle, I was eager to get something moving on this case. I hadn't developed any deep emotions over Richard Bentyne, but as a human being, I felt it ought to be worth at least as much outrage to wantonly kill one of us as it was to kill a rhino.

I said as much to Spot, a stupid habit people who live alone with animals frequently acquire. He recognized my tone of voice and made his sympathetic noise, "Moooooort," with a sort of rising inflection on the last three o's.

"Of course," I added, "if it turns out he was killed *by a rhinoceros*, we could just call the whole thing even and forget it."

But no one was going to forget, and that meant it was time to find Marcie Nast. I'd talked to an ex-roommate who said that Marcie spent every summer Monday night playing softball in Central Park. Not the long day-lit August evenings, *nights*.

Of course that made sense. Bentyne taped his show at five-thirty each weekday, it ran an hour, it was very unlikely anybody on the production staff would get out of the building before seven.

That was on a normal day, of course, and this was far from that. But it wouldn't affect the softball schedule, would it?

So the game wasn't very likely to start before eight o'clock. And though there is a virtually infinite number of places to play softball in Central Park, there are only a very few *lighted diamonds*. I could check those out in no time, and if Marcie wasn't there, I would have lost nothing but time.

I looked at my watch. Hell, I even had time to feed and water Spot and get something to eat (I suddenly realized I'd had nothing since breakfast, and discovered myself to be starving) before I started looking.

And change my clothes. That was imperative, that I change my clothes. For someone like me, six foot two a little over two hundred pounds, Central Park at night is not the horror zone it might be for a kid or a senior citizen. But there's no need to be foolhardy, either. I could enter the park wearing the Brooks Brothers three-piece suit I had on, or I could hang a sign around my neck saying RICH GUY—MUG ME FOR BIG BUCK$.

So I had my evening planned. I stopped at a Kentucky Fried Chicken and picked up dinner. I know it's sick, but I'd had the urge for it all day. Then I went home, shed the suit, put on some light sweats, white socks, and sneakers, fed Spot and myself.

I checked my answering machine, but I hardly ever got any messages at all anymore, not since I was assigned the damn cellular phone.

Then I got the leash again, and watched Spot's black eyes light up in doggy delight. If it were up to him, he'd never come indoors. Off we went, back to the park.

I found a game at the diamond up near Eighty-ninth Street; the game hadn't started yet. The sodium vapor lamps distorted color a little, but I could have sworn one of the teams was wearing pink shirts.

So they were. Pink shirts with the words *Coif You!* written on them in exquisite script. I asked somebody on the other team (pastel green shirts labeled Mr. Leonard of Soho) who the game was between.

"Hairdressers' League," he said matter-of-factly. "Staff and customers, you know. Are you in the profession?"

"No, I'm trying to catch up to a woman I thought might be here."

He looked me up and down and gave me a twisted smile.

"Oh," he said. "Well, help yourself."

"That's awfully magnanimous of you," I said.

"This is a mixed league, after all."

"Yeah," I said. "Thanks." I looked around for a while, and for a minute I thought my big deduction was a bust.

Then I saw her. I never would have spotted her if she hadn't been wearing the California Angels cap. In her glasses and shapeless sweat suit she'd looked like a nerd out to make life tedious for everybody she met. Acted that way, too. In a pink T-shirt and shorts, she was unbelievable.

Vivian Pike certainly hadn't lied—that was a bitchin' bod. Not fashion model slim, but curvy and robust, like a fifties' pinup. The face that the spectacles had made pinched and owlish was now, if not conventionally beautiful, aware and challenging.

There were two facts, one about me and one about her, that I was glad I already knew. First, I was already in love; second she was a royal pain-in-the-ass at work. If I were unattached and just laying eyes on her for the first time, I might have launched myself headlong into another of the fiascos with which my romantic past and psyche are littered.

I walked up to her. "Marcie Nast? Matt Cobb. You saw me this morning; I was talking with Vivian Pike."

She eyed me with something other than pleasure. "What are you doing here?"

"I'd like to talk to you, if you've got a minute."

"I spent the whole day talking. The Network doesn't own me, you know."

"I wasn't planning to sell you to an Arab sheikh, I wanted to ask you some questions."

"I've got no answers. Get lost." She dropped to the turf and started doing stretching exercises.

"Yes, Your Majesty." I bowed. "Do I have to leave just the park, for which I pay taxes, or the whole City of New York?"

"It's all the same to me," she said.

I was about to take matters up one level of nastiness and ask if she'd told the cops about her little dressing-room rendezvous with Bentyne (I knew she hadn't, because the lieutenant had heard it from me, and they were saving it for a later date), when a young man with eyes every bit as intense as Marcie's came up to us. He was wearing glasses. He was a little smaller than I was, but he was plenty wiry, and besides he was holding an aluminum baseball bat in his hands.

He looked at me, but addressed her. "Is he bothering you, sis?"

His voice wasn't loud, but it was peculiarly intense. I had no doubt that if she said yes, her brother would have beaten my head in without another word.

Marcie must have, too. It certainly wasn't love that led her to say, "No, Peter, everything's fine. This is Matt Cobb, somebody I know from work. He came up to watch the game."

With that, all hostility was gone. He smiled, and took one hand off the bat to shake. "Hi," he said. "I'm Peter Nast."

He told me it was a horrible thing that happened at the Network, and I agreed with him.

"Unfortunately, I don't know if there's going to be a game."

"What's the matter, Pete?" his sister asked.

"I just checked my machine. Wendell left a message. He was chopping apples for a Waldorf salad, and cut his left thumb. He was calling from the emergency room. Seven stitches. No way he can play."

"Can he work?" Marcie demanded.

Peter thought so. It turned out that Wendell was a hairdresser at Coif You!, one of the top feather-cut men in New York. The left thumb could be compensated for while cutting hair, or so Peter, the owner of Coif You! thought, but not for playing softball, especially for a catcher, which was Wendell's position on the team.

"Can't somebody else catch?" Marcie demanded angrily.

"Sure, I could do it myself, I've got the mitt and the mask, and let Sammi pitch. But we've still only got nine people."

"We can beat them with nine. We'll go without a short fielder."

"I already thought of that. Leonard is willing to go along, but Wolf is being a bastard about the rules. You know Wolf."

Leonard was Mr. Leonard of Soho. Wolf was as big as Cass Le Boudlier only even more muscular. He looked like a statue of Zeus, except that Zeus is usually depicted as having hair and a beard, while Wolf didn't have so much as a follicle visible anywhere on his body, except eyelashes. He was Leonard's partner, it seemed, both in life and in the salon. He, apparently, was the slickest and smoothest head-shaver in the Northeast, not a skill I would have thought was in great commercial demand, but you live and learn.

"He says if we field only nine players, our best hitters will get up more often over the course of the game. He wants us to forfeit," Peter concluded.

"Of course he does." Marcie could have been a spitting cobra. "That will put them a full game ahead of us with a clear run to the championship."

"I can catch," I said.

Peter was glaring at me again. It was occurring to me that being mercurial, tense, and touchy were genetic in this family. "Look, Cobb. Don't get the idea because a lot of us are gay that you're going to lord it up over a bunch of fairies. We play hard, and we're good at the game. Don't try to sign on if you can't pull your weight."

"I wouldn't dream of it," I said. "I can catch."

"Can you hit?"

"Not for power. I don't strike out much. I can bunt and hit behind the runner. In fact, I hit best to the opposite field."

I think it was the realistic assessment of my abilities that sold him. If I'd told him I was the second coming of Reggie Jackson, he would have laughed me off.

Peter screwed up his mouth. He turned to Marcie, who had stopped stretching and was standing beside him.

"What do you think, sis?"

She looked me over as if she were planning to sell *me* to an Arab sheikh.

"Fuck it," she said at last. "Bat him eighth, after me, and ahead of Hernando and Tiffany. If that bastard Wolf will go for it."

I smiled brightly. "If he does, and if we win, I'd like to buy you a drink after the game, Marcie."

She thought that one over, too. If she said no, it would confirm her brother's original assessment of my motives. If she said yes, she knew she'd wind up alone with me hearing the questions she was trying to avoid.

But I don't think either of those two things decided it. I think it was the fact that if she said no, I might not play; if I didn't play, she couldn't play; and if she couldn't play, she couldn't win.

Marcie, I was learning, was a woman hungry to win. At everything.

Wolf sneered at the idea. He had a slight accent—not the German that his name suggested. Something I couldn't place. "Bringing in a ringer, Peter? I am disappointed in you. The rules say staff and customers only."

Peter was steaming up. I cut in before he could explode. "Hey, I need a haircut, anyway. I promise tomorrow I'll go to Peter's place and have him coif me."

Wolf didn't shoot down the suggestion right away. Leonard, who looked like a young Richard Chamberlain, except with platinum blond hair, put a hand on his partner's bicep and said, "Come on, Wolf, we've all come out to the park, we've got to pay the umpire anyway, let's get the game in."

"Here's the deal. If you *win* you let Peter cut your hair tomorrow. If you lose, you let me cut your hair, right here on the field before we leave. I always carry my stuff with me."

Marcie said, "You really *are* a bastard, Wolf," investing the word bastard with all sorts of new shades of meaning. She seemed to want to go on, but I cut her off.

"It's a deal," I said.

"In some secluded rendezvous . . ."
—TONY RANDALL
The Odd Couple, ABC

13

Peter Nast had not been whistling Dixie.

I didn't know whose sexual preference was what, and I didn't care a damn. As far as softball was concerned, these were my kind of people

A lot of people play sports to socialize and work up a sweat, and I suppose for them, it's fine. For me, if I want to socialize, I'll go to a party, and if I want to sweat, I'll take up (yuck) jogging.

But to get the most out of a sport, you have to stretch yourself, to test yourself, to get the absolute best out of yourself that's there, with no compromises—not with the rules, not with the opposition, not with the demands of the game itself.

That was the way Coif You! and Mr. Leonard of Soho

played softball. I think some professional athletes could have learned from them. We slid hard to break up double plays. We went for the extra base. We knew how many outs there were, and we knew where the runners were on base. The infielders (Marcie was the shortstop—she threw like a girl, but then so did Tony Kubek. She got the ball there.) planted themselves directly in front of the grounders, and were always in position to take relays and cutoffs.

I never enjoyed a game more in my life.

We took a four–two lead into the ninth. I'd been part of two of the runs, scoring ahead of Sammi's single in the fourth, then moving Marcie from the first to third with a sacrifice bunt-and-run, after which she scored on Hernando's sacrifice fly.

Coif You! was the visiting team, so Leonard's team was batting to end the game.

With two outs and a man on, Wolf came to bat. As always, the bat looked like a twig when he held it. We'd managed to walk him every previous time he'd come up before this. It was a good strategy. He was strong enough to hit the ball out of any park in the country, Central included. Hell, he could have hit one out of Yellowstone, if he got a tail wind.

Wolf was not happy. The lights gleamed on the sweat of his muscles and the gold of his earring. "Just give me one to hit, you pussies," he said under his breath.

Fat chance, I thought, but with a count of two balls and no strikes on him, Peter made his one really bad pitch of the night, a little high, on the outside part of the plate.

Wolf crushed it.

As soon as I heard it hit, I thought, here we go, extra innings. Jono, the left fielder, was running dead away from me as though a flying saucer had landed just behind second base. The runner from first scored before he even caught up with the ball, but Wolf had just gotten to second, and I began to have some hope. I got rid of my mask and awaited developments.

Jono would have needed a howitzer to get the ball back to the infield from where he was, but he hit Hernando, the short fielder, with a perfect throw, who in turn pegged it to Marcie, who'd come out to get the relay.

Wolf, representing the tying run, was rounding third as Marcie was wheeling. I watched him from the corner of my eye, but my attention was on the ball.

"Home it! I yelled. *"Home it!"*

Marcie never had any intention of doing anything else. She threw me a perfect strike that smacked into my mitt with Wolf still about fifteen feet away.

He'd seen me catch the ball. I could tell from his eyes he wasn't going to slide, wasn't going to try to avoid the tag. Wolf probably had never slid in his life. He was going to try to bowl me over and knock the ball loose.

For a split second, I felt a cold prickle on my scalp, probably a foreshadowing of my head being shaved.

Then I got very calm, remembered my training. Ball in fist, fist in glove, glove against chest with the fist inside.

I braced myself, but that was only temporary. If all you do is brace yourself when somebody like Wolf is bearing down on you, you're likely to wake up in the hospital with footprints on your face.

It's counterintuitive, but the best thing to do is *jump into* the runner with all your might, make sure *he* soaks up some of the impact, too.

I jumped, chest first.

It was like being run over by a truck.

We both went down. Wolf recovered first, scrambled off me, and crossed the plate, screaming "Yes!"

The umpire was standing over me. Groggily, I unfolded my hands and showed him the ball. "You're out!" he hollered, pumping his hand in the air to emphasize it.

Wolf said, "What?" so hard his voice cracked, and he came over to see for himself.

"Son of a bitch!" he cried, pulling me to my feet. "Who would have believed you could hang on to that ball?"

The news finally sank in to my pink-shirted teammates, and they rushed in from the field to congratulate me, led by Spot, who had spent the game sitting like a good boy by the bench while everybody told him how beautiful he was, and especially admired his hair.

I was mobbed. There were nine other members of the Coif You! team, five of them women, but I swear I got at least seven kisses. I didn't care, I was on another plane, and I loved them all.

"*Nobody* blocks the plate on Wolf," Peter was saying. "They just play bullfighter and try to tag him as he goes by."

"Good way to break an arm," I told him.

"What you did," Marcie said, "was a good way to break your head." Then she kissed me again, going out of her way this time to make it memorable.

Peter contented himself with shaking my hand, which made me just as glad. "Don't forget to show up for the haircut tomorrow. I'll handle you personally. On the house. No. You pay, like a dollar. Or even full price, it'll be worth it—I'm the best. You'll never go anywhere else. Then you'll be a legit customer, and we can add you to the team for the rest of the season."

I held up a hand.

"Whoa," I said. "Thanks, I'm honored, but I don't know if I could commit to the rest of the season."

"It's only five more weeks," somebody said.

"Well, seven if we go all the way," another voice added.

I was beginning to feel like some high-priced free agent.

"Maybe little sister can persuade him, eh?"

"I've warned you before about your filthy mouth, Hernando," Marcie said. She sounded bored.

"Hey," I said. "I never wanted to cause dissension around here. Tell you what—when I get my hair cut tomorrow, I'll find out the rest of the details from Peter. If I can do it at all, I will. How's that?"

Peter said, "Well . . ."

"What do you want?" his sister demanded. "A contract signed in blood? Matt is an important man, he can't just close up the shop when there's a game. He said he'll do his best. Now leave him alone."

There were murmurs about how they hadn't meant to get pushy, just wanted to keep me on the team, I fit in great, etc., great game, thanks, and so on. All very gratifying. Then they drifted away, and I was alone with Spot and Marcie.

She was scratching the Samoyed behind the ears. "This your dog?"

"Sort of. Why?"

"He's too beautiful, he's like a walking fur stole. A fashion accessory. You're not the accessory type."

"How do you know what type I am? You never knew I existed until this morning."

"I knew you existed. I've made it my business to know about everybody important at the Network."

"I'm not that important."

She laughed. "You sleep with the major stockholder. That makes you important."

"That's frank," I said. I was irritated.

"I'm always frank, unless I make a conscious decision not to be."

"Good, that'll come in handy when you answer my questions."

"Sure," she said. "But not here. They'll be turning off the lights soon, and I'm holding you to that drink you blackmailed me into."

"Mmm," I agreed. "And after you saved my life tonight, too."

"Peter is very protective."

"So I noticed. Thanks."

"I didn't do it for you, I just didn't want my brother to get in trouble. Or hurt. I saw your eyes. Bat or no bat, you weren't afraid."

"Wrong. I was afraid I was going to have to have Spot rip out his throat."

"Would he?"

"On command. There's more to this fluffball than good looks."

"That's something the three of us have in common, then."

"Where do you want to have this drink? There's a place on Central Park West not too far from here, we could talk and I could put you in a cab for home after."

She put her finger on the tip of my nose. "I'll be frank again. I like you a lot better than I did before the game started. But you got me into this, and you are not getting off cheap—or the Network isn't. This will be on your expense account, won't it?"

She went on without waiting for an answer.

"And, Matt dear, you are hardly presentable. There is sweat and dust on your face, your hair is mud, and while you taste delicious, you smell like dirty socks.

"So here is what we'll do," she said primly. "You will indeed walk me to Central Park West and put me in a cab. Then you'll take a cab home yourself, make yourself presentable, and meet me in an hour and a half in the Churchill Bar."

The idea held a certain appeal. The sooner I got my Wolf-battered body into a hot shower, the better I'd like it. We could also linger longer over fewer drinks at a place like the Churchill. Hell, with what they charged for a drink you should get a month's rent with it.

"It would not," I told her, "amuse me to be stood up."

"I'll be there," she promised.

Clean, nicely dressed, and Spot-free, I sat in the cab on the way across the Park wondering if she was going to be there. I also realized I personally couldn't do much about it if she weren't, since if I tried to make her life difficult at the Network, she had a *prima facie* sexual harassment case on me a two-year-old could argue successfully. It would be a lie, but most sexual harassment complaints are definitely *not*, and that little statistic would tell against me, too.

Damned clever, our little Marcie.

Still, I had things to fall back on. If she didn't want to talk to me, she could talk to the cops. Formidable as she was, tough as she seemed, the lieutenant had a detective on his staff named Denise Berkowitz who could take Marcie apart like a peeled tangerine.

But it was academic. Marcie was there, in this case, Marcie, Mark III.

Gone was the frump of the morning; gone was the pocket Amazon of the softball diamond. In their place was the young career woman off for a carefree night on the town.

She was standing just inside the door, waiting for me, in a flower print summerweight dress that managed to show plenty of leg and back, along with a provocative shadow of cleavage, without ever losing its air of innocence. The glasses were back, but instead of making her look owlish, they made her look perky and alert.

I put myself on alert. A woman who could convincingly present three very different personae in fourteen hours was potentially dangerous. Not that most people don't put on different faces for different occasions—they do, constantly. Most of them, though, have a base personality that comes out when we let our guard down, a default

mode, as computer mavens call it. It's the thing that au-
tomatically gets done when there are no orders to do anything special.

Each of the personae I saw her in seemed to be her
default mode, but I don't think any of them was. They
were not only different, they were *alien* to each other.
Either she was acting all the time, or she had no real self
to fall back on, just another role to step into.

She saw me and said, "Well *there* you are," like a popular high school girl encouraging a shy date. "I was afraid
you were going to stand *me* up."

"Liar," I said. "No man has ever stood you up in your
life."

She looked at me for a second. "You're right," she said.
"Let's sit down."

We found a quiet booth in the corner. A waitress came
by and we ordered, a Gibson for her, Wild Turkey 101
with water back for me. One thing about the Churchill—
when the last glass of 101 is served, it will be the Churchill
that serves it. They've probably been stocking up for years.

Marcie looked at me. I could see her eyes glittering
behind her glasses. "I like you better all the time. You
have no more tolerance for bullshit than I have."

"If you can't tolerate bullshit," I told her, "you're in the
wrong business."

She showed me a rounded throat as she threw back her
head to laugh.

"Oh no," she said. "I am most emphatically in the right
business. I am bursting with ideas, I'm smart, tough, and
ruthless. I'll wind up running this Network."

I sipped bourbon.

"That's an interesting thought," I said. "Is there a time-
table on this project?"

"Not a strict one. It'll happen while I'm still young
enough to enjoy it." She rubbed a fingertip around the
rim of her glass. "You'll be there, working for me."

"Maybe," I said.

"Yes, you're right, maybe. If I decide to let you stay." She laughed deep in her throat.

"There's something I want to ask you," I said.

"Ah, yes, the famous questions."

"No, those come later. I'm still trying to figure you out."

"I'm easy to figure out," she said. With a dainty finger and thumb, she picked the onion out of her glass and crushed it between her teeth.

"You are a remarkable young woman," I said.

"Thank you."

"Watching you in action tonight, on the diamond and off, I would say you are perfectly capable of taking care of yourself."

"Perfectly capable," she echoed.

"Why does your brother come on like a hillbilly with a shotgun to protect you, then? He seemed perfectly sane the rest of the time."

She took a pull at her drink. "What you want to know is what makes *Peter* tick.

"Well, that's easy, too. Peter was eighteen, you see, just legally an adult, and I was twelve, when our mother died. Our father'd deserted us years ago, he's probably dead and I hope he is.

"Anyway, Peter kept us together. It would be hard enough for any eighteen-year-old to bring up his twelve-year-old sister—imagine the pressure on a gay eighteen-year-old."

"Peter is gay, then?"

"Don't you think so?"

"Just being a hairdresser doesn't make him gay."

"What is this, Matt? Did you think about the game and get queasy over the idea that you may have just gone through a major bonding experience with a bunch of faggots?"

"Wild pitch, Marcie. Not even close. That couldn't work unless I had some doubts about myself. I just don't like jumping to conclusions."

"And you don't have any doubts about yourself?"

"Nothing to get me queasy," I said.

"There's something else we have in common," she said. "I don't have any doubts, either."

She took another sip and went on. "This is good. Helps me relax after a game. And of course I don't have to go to work tomorrow. We spent all day putting together a "best of" tape, and tonight, News is taking the time slot for a special on the murder. Anyway to answer your question— frankly as always—I don't know if Peter *is* gay. Most of his friends and employees are, but I don't know if he is. I don't know if he's ever had a partnered orgasm in his life, and we don't discuss his fantasy life.

"You see, I'm Peter's project. He gives things up for me. He was supposed to go to college, but of course when mother died, that was out. Instead he apprenticed to a hairdresser, and turned out to be brilliant at it. Took over the place eventually. Does quite, quite well.

"The other thing he gave up for me was a sex life, normal or ab, I couldn't say. The way Peter sees New York, it's a jungle, only the predators are social workers, ready to snatch me off to a foster home at the slightest excuse. So he never gave them one."

"He must love you very much."

"Oh, he does."

"And you must be very grateful to him."

"Yes, I must, mustn't I? The closest I ever come to feeling guilty is when I realize I'm not. I just think Peter is a shmuck to do what he's done. *I* certainly wouldn't do it for anybody."

I said, "That was certainly frank."

"Told you. Next question?"

"Okay. Being as capable as you are, why do you need to

pull all that Suzie-Creamcheese victimized woman crap at work on Vivian Pike?"

"Oh. Well, that's over now. It was all part of the plan."

"What plan?"

"Matt, I don't think you've been paying attention. The plan to take over the Network. I always get what I want, Matt, and I always take the shortest safe route to getting it. The fact that everyone does it any other way has always been totally mystifying to me.

"And to get what I want, I'll use everything I can— lawsuits and court decisions, people's illusions and misconceptions, my own brains and talent, anything.

"Surely you can see that Vivian Pike was an obstacle to me? I don't want other women with power around the Network. It will detract from my own uniqueness. Women subordinates I can handle; they'll be a power base. Women equals or superiors?"

She shook her head. "They've got to go. Do you think I could have another Gibson?"

I flagged the waitress and took care of it. I was glad of the chance to take a breath. The woman was a psychopath. I felt like the stenographer for *Mein Kampf*. Except of course that the stenographer for *Mein Kampf* was Joseph Goebbels, and he was just as crazy as Hitler was.

The drink came. She took another ladylike sip and approved of it.

"Everything you can," I said. "Does that include screwing Bentyne in his dressing room every afternoon?"

"Naturally."

So much for my big gun.

"It was even enjoyable, a little. He was so eager to please. Richard may have been a terrific entertainer, but he was dreadfully insecure."

"And this was part of the plan."

"Matt, you don't have to be deliberately obtuse." She was getting genuinely irritated.

"Humor me," I said. "The Network's paying."

"That's true. All right, I'll spell it out, but honestly! By fucking Richard, I simultaneously bound him to me, and drove a wedge between him and Vivian. Her entire power base was her relationship with Richard—not that he'd touched her in almost a year, anyway—anxiety about the Network deal."

She looked puzzled. "That's another thing I'll never understand—why do people get *anxiety* when they should be feeling *triumph?*"

"Crossed wires in the psyche," I offered.

"You could be right. It's the best explanation I've ever heard for it."

She waved it away. "So there was that, and there was the fact that she was doing a good job as a producer. Her weakness there was that she felt pressure too much. So I did everything I could to put more pressure on her."

She smiled at me. "Did you really need me to explain all that?"

"I guess not," I said. "What are you going to do now? No more show, no more job."

"I'll get reassigned somewhere. If the Network doesn't place me quickly enough, or tries to fob me off with some Sunday afternoon public affairs show nobody watches, I'll go back to court. I'm not worried."

She tilted her head. "I'm more worried about you."

"Me?"

"Yeah. Like, should I seduce you, or not. You'd undoubtedly be better in bed than Richard was, you might even make me come."

"Don't flatter yourself. Besides, I don't have access to rhino horn,"

Marcie laughed, loud. "Wasn't that *pathetic?* How did you know? Did you find his stash?"

"A cop did," I said.

She sighed as the laugh subsided. "Poor Richard. But you know, it did help him. Strictly psychological, I'm sure. Like Dumbo's magic feather."

"He just kept remembering that rhinos stay coupled for forty-five minutes at a time." That was a piece of knowledge I'd picked up earlier that evening from Bill Bevacqua's tapes.

"But not with their horns," she said.

"Good point," I said.

"And as for flattering myself, I never do. I could have you in bed tonight, if I wanted to. You'd love it. But the question is, what would be the point of making an enemy of Roxanne Schick? She's not a threat to me at present, and since it would be a lot of work to neutralize her, I think I won't go out of my way to antagonize her."

"I don't make love unless I'm in love," I told her.

"How corny."

"I don't picture myself in love with you."

She shrugged. "Maybe not. I think it bothers you to meet a woman as smart as you are, but tougher and more honest with herself. See, my theory is nobody really cares about anybody else. They just bog themselves down in pretending to."

"I see. Everybody does what you do; you just do it better because you do it consciously."

"Exactly!" she said, as if to a bright pupil. "I knew you were smart. It's very liberating. I'm complimenting you when I say I think you could get there if you worked at it a little." She laughed again, so loud that other people turned to look at us. "Together, we could rule the world!"

"You realize this kind of talk does not serve to remove you from suspicion for Bentyne's murder."

"Don't be absurd. What possible motive could I have?"

"He might have kissed you off."

"And gotten himself a big stink of publicity after I talked to my lawyer and the press. Not that there was any danger of it happening, Matt. He was deliriously happy with me.

"Besides, murder is stupid. It's so . . . *irrevocable*. There are so many other, better ways to deal with difficult people. The odds against murder are too high; and the other ways don't have long prison sentences attached to them if you make a mistake. I wouldn't kill anybody, Matt. I'm too smart to. I'm too smart to need to."

I believed her. I also believed this decision had been thought over long and hard before the murder option had been rejected as a matter of policy. I told her as much.

"I think long and hard about everything," she said primly.

"Okay," I said. "Drink up. It's late, and I, at least, still have to go to work tomorrow."

She did. "I hope I've been helpful," she said. "You worked so hard to earn it, after all."

"Come on," I said, "I'll put you in a cab. We wouldn't want that remarkable brain of yours spilled all over the sidewalk by a mugger, would we?"

"You don't sound as if you've made up your mind on the question yet," she said.

"No? I have, though."

I flagged a taxi, told him the address, and handed him ten dollars of the Network's money.

I opened the back door for Marcie. Before she got in, she grabbed me by the ears, pulled my face down to hers, and planted another enthusiastic kiss on me.

When she took her mouth away, she said, "Any time I wanted you," then closed the door and disappeared into the night.

"Look, it says right here,
'PRIVATE PROPERTY—NO FISHING ALLOWED.' "
"No it doesn't, it says, 'PRIVATE PROPERTY?
NO! FISHING ALLOWED!' "
—LEE CHAMBERLIN AND RITA MORENO
The Electric Company, PBS

14

When your Monday has consisted of a murder, two sessions with a boss who doesn't like you, a trip to the country, the chase and capture of a fleeing man, a tough softball game, and a *tête à tête* with a beautiful psycho who more or less announces that at a more convenient time and place for her she intends to have your body, whatever it will do to your life, it tends to bode ill for the rest of the week.

That was why I didn't go bounding with enthusiasm into Tuesday. I took it nice and slow, like a man getting into a too-hot tub.

Before I'd even gotten into bed Tuesday morning (about 2 A.M.) I'd rung the Network and left a message on Jazz's machine that I wouldn't be in until after lunch.

Then I slept till ten-thirty (I am convinced that every second of sleep you get past eight hours prolongs your life). I got up, had a nice bowl of Kellogg's Corn Pops (known in my youth as Sugar Corn Pops, before sugar became a dirty word), read *The New York Times*, and only then decided to get dressed.

Reading the *Times* had been a mistake anyway since it was all there, all over the front page, plus an assessment of Bentyne's "legacy" on the entertainment page.

I skipped that article. His legacy to me was taking the shape of a giant pain in the ass.

Thoroughly depressed, I called my beloved on the phone and caught her between sessions.

"I miss you," I said. "When are you coming home?"

"The thing wraps up here tomorrow night. I'll be back Thursday morning."

"I can hardly wait."

There must have been something in my voice, because she said, "Is there something wrong, Matt? Is the Bentyne mess getting to you? If you need me, I'll leave right now."

"I always need you, but you stay there." It was flattering to think that she'd bag the conference if I asked her to, but I knew I would be one sorry excuse for a boyfriend if I did ask. After bouncing around to a dozen schools and earning a poker-hand full of masters's degrees, she'd finally settled down, worked hard, and was beginning to build a sizable reputation in American History between the War of 1812 and the Civil War, and this conference was a major recognition of her achievements.

"You stay there," I said again. "I can hold out for two more days. I just miss some sane company."

"Spot is perfectly sane," she reminded me.

"True, but he's a lousy conversationalist. Anyway, I just wanted to hear your voice."

"Boy," she said, "you must be in love."

"I am. You're the one who proved it to me, remember?"

"So I did. I like it."

"Me, too."

We got soppier than that before we hung up the phones, but I'll spare you. When you're in love, that kind of conversation seems perfectly natural at the time, but it looks immensely risible to outsiders.

Anyway, having recharged my emotional batteries, I took Spot for a walk in the park and cleaned up after him. Then I let him run a little while, not long enough to suit him. Spot is a wonderful dog, but he's easy to spoil. Any good thing that happens to him becomes a precedent, which he expects repeated for all time. Yesterday, he'd spent a couple of long sessions in the park, so why not today?

I had to call him three times before he came back to me. Shocking insubordination. He sulked going back to the apartment but too bad for him. I left him plenty of food and water, and plunged out into the metropolis.

The first place I plunged was one block west, to Columbus Avenue, which in recent decades turned from a slum into a sort of Greenwich Village of the North. This was where Peter Nast owned and operated Coif You!

You wouldn't think a storefront done up in silver and pink could be tasteful as well as striking, but this one was. I went inside and found Hernando behind a desk in a clean shop T-shirt (which reminded me there was a sweaty one in my hamper at home) reading *Metal Hurlant* comics in the original French.

I said, "Hello, Hernando."

He looked up at me and grinned, showing a right upper canine of gold with a diamond implanted in it. Had to be a cap—that was a regular tooth, last night.

Instead of addressing me, he called back over his shoulder, "Peter, you owe me five bucks! The hero showed up after all!"

There was general laughter from what I guess you could

call the cutting room. Hernando led me back past women and men in various states of styling. One of them said, "Hello, Mr. Cobb," and I stopped a second to say hello to the new ingenue from *Agony of Love,* the Network's top-rated soap opera.

Of the production known as Coif You, Peter Nast was not only the proprietor, he was also the Star, and as such had his own studio, a miniature version of the big room outside, plus a little corner set off as a kind of living room—black leather recliner, matching love seat, big screen TV and VCR, currently playing *Indiana Jones and the Last Crusade.*

Peter stood up to greet me, stopped the tape, and turned off the screen.

"I'm so glad you came," he said.

"I gave my word. Besides, I need a haircut."

Besides me, Hernando went, "Tsk, tsk, tsk. We don't do haircuts at Coif You! Especially Peter doesn't. You are going to get a work of art to wear on your head."

Peter laughed, and said, "That's enough, Hernando. Don't you have anything to do?"

Hernando raised an eyebrow and said, "Peter has threatened to cut all our throats if we pester you with questions about the murder."

"Good," I said. "I don't know anything, anyway." Hernando sniffed his disbelief and walked away.

"Now," Peter said. "I've been thinking about you all morning."

That sounded ominous. "You have?"

"Yes, your bone structure. And your personality. Despite what Hernando says, what we do here isn't about us, it's about our clients. We want something that suits you, that you can live with."

I acknowledged the truth of that. "I couldn't live without my head," I told him.

"You see?" he said triumphantly. "Your personality.

Obviously, you're a good-looking man, you've never worried too much about your hair. In fact, you're a little embarrassed to be here, especially since Doris recognized you."

"You saw that, huh?"

"I keep up with what's going on," he told me. "So you don't want anything too obviously styled, and you don't want anything that takes a lot of maintenance."

"Maintenance?"

"Setting, color touch-ups, blow drying, like that."

I was beginning to wonder what I'd let myself in for. "Uh, no. None of that. If you can avoid it."

"I have to avoid it. You wouldn't do it, would you?"

"Probably not."

"Definitely not. It's not your personality. So if I gave you a style that demanded those things, I would be failing you, and failing in my job. So just trust me, and we'll do fine."

Trust me, as Roxanne once pointed out to me, was what you said to somebody before you fucked them. I was beginning to think I might have been better off with Wolf and the razor cut.

After a shampoo, I was escorted royally, my head wrapped in a towel, to the chair in front of the lighted mirrors. Peter whipped off the towel, and looked at the wet mess that was my head the way Michelangelo must have approached a piece of marble, a none too flattering comparison, come to think of it.

He said, "Yes," tentatively, then spun me around and looked again. Then he said "Yes!" decisively, and his scissors started to flash in the light.

"So," he said, with the blades snipping scant millimeters from my right ear, "I hope you didn't keep my sister out too late last night."

Then I was sure I should have thrown myself on the

mercy of Wolf. Under ordinary circumstances, I might have told Peter it was none of his business, or that his sister would have to be the judge of what was too late, but over the years I had grown very attached to my ears. Furthermore, I intended never to be alone with his sister ever again, if I could help it.

So I just told him the truth. "I put her in a cab about quarter after one."

"That's not bad at all. You're a gentleman, Matt."

"I try to be."

"I worry about her. It's corny, but I can't help it."

He should worry about her, I thought. Someday, she's going to scare someone less scrupulous than I, and he's just going to kill her.

I didn't say that, of course. I said, "I'm a big brother too."

"It's a terrible way for it to happen, but I'm glad that thing with Bentyne is over. That was bad."

Scissors still snipped.

"I wish she'd settle down," he said.

Jesus, I thought, now he's trying to fix me up with her.

I was beginning to be sorry I ever walked onto that softball field, investigation or no investigation, but Peter let it lie, apparently figuring a word to the wise was sufficient. We talked about sports for the rest of the haircut; Peter was very knowledgeable, though, as a Mets fan, understandably glum. It was my sovereign right as a Yankee fan to lord it over him and his team's misfortunes, but I stifled myself in honor of having been his teammate the night before, and in the pursuit of a rapid exit.

He finished cutting and whipped out a blow dryer.

"I thought we weren't going to use one of these," I said.

"Oh, this is just for me," he responded over the roar of the machine. "You just let your hair dry naturally."

Then he was done, and I looked at myself in the mirror.

I looked great.

I don't spend a lot of time worrying about my looks, but I looked absolutely great.

My hair didn't looked styled; it didn't in fact, look all that different from the way I usually wear it. It just looked *better.*

"This is terrific," I said. "What do I owe you?"

He waved it off. "This one's on the house just like I promised. I'm pretty pleased with the way it turned out, myself. Just wash and comb it as you usually do, and see me again in about, oh, five weeks. Then you'll pay just like everyone else."

"That soon?"

He smiled, the expert talking to the tyro. "If you were on the air on the Network, instead of behind the scenes, I'd have you in here every three weeks. In five weeks, the proportionate lengths of the various parts of the hair on your head will be changed, and you won't look just right anymore."

"I never knew a hairc—I mean a styling could make so much difference."

"Just between us, I give you permission to say haircut. If you really want to show your appreciation, turn up at the Ninety-Second Street diamond in Riverside Park on Monday night."

I told him I would do my best to be there, which was almost certainly a lie, but I didn't stop to analyze it. I just got back out on the street as quickly as I could.

My secretary smiled me some Cuban sunshine as I walked in. "There you are," she said. "Gee, Matt, you look nice today."

I grinned.

"Mr. Bates has been waiting here to see you," she said. "I put him in Shirley's office." Shirley Arnstein was my other top person, on a par with Harris Brophy. She was down in Atlanta getting some things straight about our Olympic coverage.

"What the hell," I said irritably. "Send him down to Public Relations or something."

"I tried that, but he wouldn't go along. He says he's shy around people, and he trusts you. Was he really a hermit for thirty-five years? No phone, no TV, no radio, no newspapers or magazine?"

"That right."

She shuddered. "Imagine being in America with all that stuff available and not using any of it."

I laughed at her, but I agreed with her. It was like being an anorexic at a banquet. Still, a big part of freedom is the right *not* to do or have things if you didn't want to. I was just glad this country still had enough space for people like Bates to go and do what they wanted to without bothering the rest of us.

That didn't mean I was enthralled with the idea of stopping in the middle of everything I was doing to baby-sit him, either. On the other hand, if I refused to see him, God knew what he'd do, but mouthing off to the first ten reporters he came across was a good possibility.

After careful consideration, I decided the nuisance of dealing with Bates now was less than the nuisance of hearing Falzet moan about another Public Relations fiasco would be.

As a matter of fact, I didn't want to be in Falzet's vicinity at all, now that the rhino horn business had broken. The *Times* that morning had been full of it, and animal rights groups had been picketing the building as I came in. It occurred to me that it would have been more impressive from a media point of view, and also more to the point, if a bunch of *rhinos* had been picketing the building, but I supposed that would have been kind of tough to organize.

I often indulge in whimsy to avoid thinking about things

that irk me. I made myself stop. That's just fighting the problem, instead of solving it.

It wouldn't be fighting the problem, I told myself cunningly, if I were to gather more information before facing Bates. He was bound to ask questions. Besides, it was a good idea to let the cops know I was about to converse with a fellow suspect. It was my duty as a citizen. While I was at it, I would tell them about my talk with Marcie, another suspect, and apologize for how my duty as a citizen had managed to slip my mind in that instance.

I picked up the phone and called Lieutenant Martin's direct number. Rivetz answered.

"Waddaya want, Cobb?" he demanded, recognizing my voice.

"The lieutenant around?"

"Nah, he's upstairs with the deputy commissioner. Probably getting his ass handed to him over your precious Network star. Will I do?"

I told him he would.

"Good. Funny, isn't it, how the rhino story leaked before we broke it down here?"

"Astounding how these things happen," I said.

"Yeah," he said. "Good word. Astounding. Seriously, I hope it did you some good to break it first. I just hope it turns down the heat on us."

"Is anybody picketing at Police Plaza?"

"There's *always* some assholes picketing at Police Plaza. I think the architect planned them in. But is anybody bitching about this case in particular? No."

"Then you're already ahead. We've got pickets."

That perked him up a little. I took advantage of his relative good humor to give him a fairly detailed account of my conversation with Marcie last night.

When I finished, he let out a low whistle.

"Oh, Cobb, you poor bastard, you've got this gorgeous bimbo grabbing for your bod."

"Rivetz, believe me when I say that gorgeous she may be, but that I would personally rather go to bed with an electric hedge trimmer. On."

"Yeah," he conceded. "I read the transcript of her interviews. I was going to accuse the detective of being a frustrated pulp writer and making her up."

"No, if it's scary and weird, it's probably Marcie all right. Now," I said, "I've got another eccentric to deal with. Clement Bates has been waiting around three hours to see me."

"So see him," Rivetz said. "I got my own troubles."

"Anything you want me to tell him? Anything I should avoid telling him?"

"Why?"

"Well, he's a suspect, isn't he?"

"Cobb, do you really see our backwoodsman as the perp here?"

"No."

"Why not?"

"No conceivable motive. Lack of knowledge necessary to do it. I mean, sure, he had opportunity to wander around the theater to his heart's delight, and for the sake of argument, he might even have had a kilo of Deth-on-Ratz concealed about his person. He could have been able to get intimate with the chicken—"

"*Anybody* could have gotten intimate with the chicken, as it turns out. Your driver, Gambrelli, got to flirting with a script girl, and that picnic hamper thing wound up sitting on a table in a side room, unwatched, for a good fifteen minutes."

"Even so. Bates wasn't a regular—he didn't know that the chicken was going to be there."

"Yeah," Rivetz conceded. "That's the way we read it

around here. The only way he could have known about it was to read it off the computer up at Bentyne's place, and spending thirty-five years in the boonies, that's one skill he's going to lack."

"So I can talk to him?"

"You can marry him, for all I care. It's only a formality we're making him hang around the city. Doesn't look right if we start letting 'suspects' go back to hiding on their mountains."

"I think I'm also going to want to have a chat with Vivian Pike."

"A real suspect, this time."

"Yeah. I won't blow your case for you."

"The lieutenant wouldn't let you live long, if you did. He'd tell your mother on you. Listen, to talk to this Pike woman, you've got to find her first, right?"

"Absolutely."

"Well, officially, I'm supposed not to want you to find her, so I'm telling you, whatever you do, don't look for her at the house in Darien, even if the Network does own it. Got me?"

"I got you."

It occurred to me that this was the most helpful and the least snotty Rivetz had ever been to me. Maybe personal troubles had mellowed him.

"One thing about this Bates guy, before we hang up," he said. "With all his eccentricity, he's kind of boring, you know? I had a session with himself myself. No wonder that guy gave up on his book.

"Something we turned up in a background check. Freelance writer named Frank Harlan was trying to sell a book on Bates about three years ago. No takers."

"Bates mentioned something about it. Still might be worth talking to Harlan, though."

"We will, when we find him. Guy apparently writes his

way around the world and back. Tough life, huh? Those writer guys have it made."

I reflected for a moment on how nice it would be to be working on a laptop by the side of a loch in Scotland about now, eating smoked salmon, with the temperature about twenty degrees cooler than it was in New York.

I was doing it again.

I brought myself back to the present and said, "Listen, Rivetz, I hope everything works out okay for you."

He was gruff. "Yeah, thanks. I had no business dumping all my troubles on you."

"Forget it," I said.

"Hey, Cobb," he said brightly. "What do you do when your nose goes on strike?"

"What?"

"Picket!" He laughed and hung up.

I hit the intercom and told Jazz to send in Bates.

He materialized like a genie—I hardly noticed the door open, then there he was, medium-sized, scruffy-bearded, and wearing the same suit and string tie he'd had on Friday evening.

He stood in front of my desk and sized me up.

"Nice haircut," he said.

I was starting to feel self-conscious. "What can I do for you, Mr. Bates?"

"What can you do for me? I'm going stir crazy in that silken prison they call a hotel."

"I thought you were used to being by yourself. Sit down, by the way."

"What? Oh, sure." He picked a chair and sat. "Hell, I like to be by myself, but I'm used to being able to walk thirty miles while I'm doing it. I'm not used to staring at four walls, no matter how much food they'll bring me."

"Nobody's stopping you from walking, Mr. Bates," I said.

"I thought you were gonna call me Clem," he said. "Or was that only when I was gonna be a TV star?"

Actually, I'd been hoping he'd forgotten. "Of course, not, Clem. But you can walk to your heart's content."

"No I can't. You say there's nobody stopping me from walking, but the truth is, millions of people are stopping me. All of them, out there, all the ants on the New York anthill, they're stopping me. I can barely get a good stride going, and there's somebody cutting me off. I'm going nuts, and I thought that since you're the one responsible for getting me out here—"

"Hey," I said, "I didn't invite you to be on Bentyne's show, and I didn't send him the letter saying you'd do it."

"You picked me up at the dad-blamed airport."

I was silent. In the face of that kind of logic, words were powerless. Besides, he wasn't done yet.

"And don't try to fob me off on the 'Network.' The Network don't have a face, and your face is the only one I know." He added, not quite under his breath, "Everything would have been fine, if Bentyne hadn't been killed."

"I didn't do that either," I said.

I was trying to think of a way to explain to him that I didn't have the time to wet nurse him, no matter how insecure his years in the wilderness had made him among people.

Then the phone rang, and I grabbed for it like a man crawling across the Sahara would grab a Popsicle.

"What is it, Jazz?"

"A Ms. Vivian Pike, on line two."

"No kidding," I said. "Put her on, Jazz."

A click, and there she was. I gave her my best corporate phone style, a crisp, "Matt Cobb."

"Mr. Cobb, this is Vivian Pike. We met yesterday."

The last part of that could have been false modesty—I wasn't likely to have forgotten anybody I'd met in connection with the Bentyne show yesterday—but it didn't sound that way. Yesterday, I'd noticed how Vivian Pike's voice seemed to be dead. Today it had some emotion in it. It was the voice of someone cringing against further blows.

"I remember, Miss Pike. What can I do for you?"

"I want to talk to you," she said.

That was convenient, I thought.

"In person," she added. "I—I don't want to talk to you about this on the phone. I don't trust phones."

"Do you want to meet somewhere?"

"Oh," she said. There was silence for a few seconds. Then she said, "I know this is a terrible imposition, but would you mind coming to me? I had such a time getting to—where I am without the press tracking me. Could you—"

"I know where you are, Miss Pike. I'll be with you in, oh, an hour or an hour an a half, depending on the traffic on 95."

"Thank you," she said. "I know you'll have to tell the police what I have to tell you, but maybe you can handle it in some way that won't be as terrible for me as I deserve. I don't think I can handle anything anymore."

My God, I thought, she's going to confess to murder.

"Sit tight," I said, "I'll be right there."

She thanked me again. I hung up and started to brush off Bates, but he was having none of it.

"Great," he said. "Let's go."

"You can go wherever you want,"I told him, "but not with me."

"That's what you think," he told me. Then he told me I was going to Connecticut to see Vivian Pike. I'd mentioned her name, and I'd mentioned Route 95. Me and my big mouth. Then he told me he wanted to offer his condolences, and he hadn't had a chance to. With a killer running around he wanted to importune the cops up there to give him back his gun.

"And lastly," he said, "up there they've got something that can pass for woods. Maybe I can breathe a little."

I had little difficulty resisting these arguments, but when he said if I ran out on him, he'd make a beeline for the nearest reporter, my only choice was to kill him, lock him up, or take him along.

The first two had their attractions, but I reluctantly decided against them.

"Let's go," I said.

". . . Ring! Ring! Your bell will ring,
that's my very special ring,
and this is what I'll bring . . ."
—RAY HEATHERTON
The Merry Mailman (syndicated)

15

"Well," Bates said as we approached the entrance
to the house Richard Bentyne had for a short time called
home, "she must be eager to see you."

"Why?" I asked.

"Ain't that her in the road, waiting by the driveway?"

I squinted a little and saw that it was. She was leaning
against the mailbox with the sun beaming down on her
straw-colored hair. She looked as slim and sad as a scare-
crow.

"Okay," I said. "She's not expecting you; she's not going to want to deal with you. You stay in the car."

"Ha! I came out here to get a little uncitified air.
Damned if I'm going to sit in a car. You take care of
your business; I'll wander around in the woods and com-

mune with nature and breathe some semi-fresh air. You can tell her I'm here thinking of buying the house or something."

"What?"

"Well, you've got to sell it, don't you? What' the Network need with a house this far from the city? You sure aren't going to get your next big star living here. Who wants to live in a murdered man's house? So your Network is going to have to sell it to some idit with more money than he knows what to do with. I'm not an idjit, of course, but I don't mind pretending to be one, long as it's in a good cause."

"Bates," I said calmly, "she loved the guy. She lived with him. The body hasn't even been released for burial. I am not going to give the poor woman the impression that the Network is about to sell the roof from over her head or the very chairs out from under her ass!"

Bates shrugged. "Suit yourself. When I practiced it, business was business."

"Maybe everybody's better off you like it up there on your mountaintop."

That cracked him up. If I ever chuck the Network job and go into stand-up comedy, I thought, I was going to have to bring this guy around with me as a one-man claque.

"How did you know the Network owned the house?" I said.

"The man lived with me for a month, remember? He told me things."

And that would have to do, because there we were. I got the nose of the Network car off the main road and onto the gravel of the driveway.

Vivian Pike approached the car. I hit a power button and lowered the window, and the hot August air spilled into the air-conditioned car. Bates wanted to breathe this stuff? It was so thick and humid you could dish it out with a ladle.

I unlocked the back door on her side and told her to hop in. She did so, and I got the AC locked safely in again.

"I—I, uh, wasn't expecting Mr. Bates."

"Don't you worry, darlin', I've got nothing to do with this except to offer my sincere condolences. Mr. Cobb's just been kind enough to humor an old man with a ride in the country. I was going crazy in New York. Felt cooped up."

"I know what you mean," she said. "I feel cooped up everywhere. The mail didn't come till now"—she held up a half-dozen envelopes and a small paddled mailer for me to see in the rearview mirror—"but I've been down there a half-dozen times this morning. This last time, not only was the mail there but I saw one of the big, black Network-type cars coming, and I thought it must be you. I hung around to make sure. And it was you."

She committed an attempted smile. It was painful to see. She gave up, muttered, "I probably won't even open the goddamn mail," and spent the rest of the short trip staring out the window in silence.

I kept expecting Bates to ask her when she was planning to move out so he could take over the place in time for prowler-hunting season or something. Miraculously, though, having said exactly the right thing off the bat, he continued the miracle by thereafter shutting up. Maybe he could stay down from the mountain, after all.

We left Bates leaning against the car, taking deep lung-fuls of disgusting, pollen-laden summer country air while Vivian Pike led me inside to the air-conditioned comforts of civilization. She dumped the mail on a table near the front door, said, "What the hell, it's all for Richard anyway," then asked me to sit down.

I did. She kind of stood there, looking miserable. She was not acting like the high-powered producer of a Network TV show. She was a combination of a lost child and a bewildered senior citizen, though at the moment, she looked a lot more like the latter.

Her face brightened with sudden inspiration.

"Would you like something to drink? Tea? Coffee? Something stronger?"

"Mineral water would be nice if you've got some. Seltzer, you know."

"Sure. Ice? Lime?"

"Both, thanks."

"And what about Mr. Bates, he must be thirsty. I'll just call him and ask him—"

"He'll be fine," I cut in. "He came out for some isolation. If he gets thirsty, he chews tree bark."

She went and got a couple of seltzers. Or expensive mineral waters. I can tell Coke from Pepsi, but I can't tell those apart.

She folded her long legs and perched on the edge of a chair ready to jump. She took tiny little sips of her drink. Obviously, she was willing to sit there, staring and sipping, indefinitely.

She needed a nudge.

"There was something you wanted to tell me," I said.

"It's hard."

"The harder it is to tell, the more trouble will build up between now and the time it gets found out. And have no doubt that whatever it is, it'll be found out."

"I know. And that's why I'm going to tell you. But I want you to work on this for me."

"I'm working on it already."

"No. Special Projects keeps embarrassing things from becoming known. I want to be your personal special project."

"I can't promise that."

"Why not? It's your job, isn't it?"

"My job is protecting the Network. Look, suppose you were about to confess you killed Richard Bentyne. If I kept that quiet, not only would I be doing the Network a disservice I'd be putting myself in danger of spending a long, long time in a jail not of my choice."

She laughed. It wasn't genuine laughter, and it wasn't even hysteria, which, considering the state she was in, might have been a good idea—if anybody had ever been ready for a good emotional debauch, it was Vivian Pike. Unfortunately, this was a bitter little screech of hopeless irony with not an atom of humor or despair or anything human about it.

"Killed Richard," she sighed. "Oh, it would have been simpler if I had."

"Simpler?"

"Sure. If I'd killed him, I could just confess and take my chances. You don't know what my life was like. If there were enough women on the jury I might even get off."

She said, "Richard . . ." and stopped.

I thought she was going to go on and tell me what her life was like, another catalog, no doubt, of tabloid-ready atrocities—whips, chains, butterscotch pudding, that sort of thing.

As I'd said, it would come out eventually. So I braced myself.

But she surprised me. Whatever she'd been about to spill, she choked it off. Instead, she said, "No I didn't kill Richard. He made me crazy, but I didn't hate him. I even kind of still loved him."

"That's not what you got me out here to tell me."

"No, of course it isn't." She took her eyes from mine and looked around. She noticed her drink as if it had just appeared in her hand by magic. She raised it to her mouth and took a good long swallow. "I'm just trying to *explain*," she said.

"I still don't know what you're trying to explain," I said. "Or what you're trying to explain about it."

"You're right," she said decisively. "You're right, you're right. Here's what I'm trying to say."

Then she took another drink and I almost jumped on her and strangled her.

Fortunately for both of us she went on before I could act on the impulse. I could feel the muscles in my legs relaxing.

"If I'd killed him, I'd be in trouble. I'd be arrested, stand trial, maybe go to jail. Maybe for a long time."

"Probably," I said, although I knew that the average convicted murderer in New York does nine years or less actual prison time.

"There's no doubt about it," she said. "It would be a serious inconvenience."

I'm pretty good at knowing when I'm having my leg pulled, and this certainly sounded like one of those times, but Vivian Pike showed none of the signs, not in voice, face, or body language. I stared at her. I had to stare at someone who regarded a murder conviction, even a mere nine years' worth of a murder conviction, as nothing more than a "serious inconvenience."

If my staring bothered her, she showed no sign of it. She went on without missing a beat.

"—Definitely a serious inconvenience, but I could *handle* it, because it wouldn't affect me where it really matters."

"Where's that?"

"In the business. In the circles of power. You see, if I'd murdered Richard, I would have been a good producer who let personal things get to her. But if what I actually did gets out, I'll be destroyed utterly. I won't even leave a reputation behind. The very mention of my name will be forbidden."

At last we come to it, I thought. "What did you do?" I asked quietly.

Silence. After about fifteen seconds, she said, "It's hard."

I stood up. "Nope," I said. "That's where I got on this merry-go-round, and one time is enough. You'll tell the cops. Thanks for the drink," I said, and began to guzzle the rest of my seltzer.

"I gave Richard the rhino horn," she said softly.

If there were ever a time for a Danny Thomas spit-take, this was it, but I heroically kept the seltzer inside my body, mainly by swallowing it in one frozen rush that sloshed like an iceberg into my stomach.

I caught my breath, and tried to force my eyes from perfect circles into something like normal shape.

"*You* gave him the rhino horn?"

She nodded miserably. "Can't you see why I need your help? If it get out I was mixed up with rhinoceros horn, I'll be through in the business."

She sure would be, I thought. She'd had it sized up perfectly. Killing Bentyne would do her a tenth as much harm as this would.

I refrained with difficulty from ruminating on the standards of a business wherein the murder of a human being is seen as a regrettable lapse of judgment, whereas fourth- or fifth-hand participation in the products of the death of a beast was an unforgivable sin. Not that I'm in favor of poaching rhinos, mind you. I just think human beings ought to count for just as much, somehow.

"Why," I said, "did you give it to him?"

"It was an insult. I wanted to shame him. He'd just taken up with that little bitch Marcie Nast. Or rather I'd just found out about it. I was hurt, and I wanted to hurt him back. So I gave him the rhino horn, said he'd need it, because his new little playmate wouldn't be as patient with his sexual failings as I was."

"What did he say?"

"He said his sexual failings—as I called them— were all due to a lack of inspiration from me."

"So you spat in his face, kicked him in the nuts, told him to shove his show up his ass, and walked out on him, right?"

The tears that had been hovering all afternoon decided to descend. *"No,"* she said. "You know I didn't. Of course not. How could I? The *show* was just getting started. It was what we'd worked on for years. I couldn't walk out on it then. I couldn't even stop living with him—with the premiere coming up, I couldn't have the press asking the wrong kind of questions, could I?"

I was exasperated. "Does the phrase 'self-respect' mean anything to you?"

"Huh? Yes, you know it does. That's why I need your help now. What kind of self-respect can I have if this gets out?"

Forget it, Matt, I told myself, just forget it. In a million years, you aren't going to understand it.

"I'll ask," I said, "an easier question. Where did you get the stuff to give it to him?"

Mentally, I was already working angles. If the Network can help . . . who? The EPA? The United Nations? The Sierra Club? Whoever. If we could help the people in charge of rhino protecting smash a poaching ring or something, that would go a long way toward lifting the stink the late Mr. Bentyne had dumped us into. Furthermore, if Vivian Pike got immunity as some sort of anonymous witness, she might hold on to whatever illusion she thought was self-respect.

Then she said, "Oh, I had it."

This was too much. "You *had* it? You just *had* it? What, you bought it from the Avon lady and just hadn't a chance to get around to using it before? How the hell do you just happen to *have* a half a pound of rhino horn knocking around the house?"

"Oh, years ago, in L.A. I was a local news producer, and the network news was doing a big series on animal poaching in Africa, and we did a local tie-in. We worked contacts in the Asian community, and we bought the rhino horn, and a leopard skin, and some absolutely disgusting stuff from a bear's gall bladder or something. We threw the bear stuff down the toilet, and the leopard skin we gave to a museum, but I didn't know what to do with the powder. I just sort of . . . had it."

I stood up again. "All right," I said. "The cops don't have to know about this, yet."

She got up and ran to me and took my arms. "Oh, Matt," she said. It was the first time she'd called me Matt. "I'll make it up to you somehow."

"Don't thank me yet. I'm going to have your story checked—discreetly—by my West Coast people. Then we'll see."

"I'll trust your judgment."

She didn't have much choice, but I didn't say that, I just said thanks.

I'd made it to the front door now; she'd come with me, as though loath to let me go. Then she realized it, and turned to the table where she'd left the mail. She was just slipping a letter opener under the flap of the paddled mailer as I left.

Bates saw me coming and said howdy. I was about ten yards across the lawn toward the car when he looked up. Vivian Pike's voice came from behind me, calling "Matt?" and I turned just in time to see the doorway become a rectangle of red flames and black smoke, followed by a roaring noise that shot the woman off the porch and through the air like a missile.

"That's the end of *this* suit!"
—BERNIE KOPELL
When Things Were Rotten, ABC

16

I ran to her. She was unconscious by the time I
got there, which was a mercy, because she was also on fire.
I skinned out of my suit jacket, and began beating at the
flames.

She was lying face down. Her hair seemed to be burning
the worst, so I concentrated on that, slapping at it again
and again with the blue pinstriped worsted.

I looked at Bates. The man was literally dumbfounded,
standing there round-eyed, saying, "But how . . .? But
how . . .?"

It must have been the corrupting influence of the city,
I decided. If he acted that way in the mountains when a
crisis came up, he would have been grizzly chow long ago.

"Bates," I said, still flapping. The hair was pretty well

out now. I started working on the blouse and jeans. *"Bates!"*

He pulled his eyes from the flames and looked at me. "Huh?" he said.

I gave it to him loud and slow, like a man talking to a mental defective.

"Go inside," I said. "Find a phone. Call 911. Tell them we've got a badly burned woman here, and we need an ambulance right away. Do you remember the address?"

He recited it for me, then ran inside.

I got rid of the flames. Vivian Pike's skin, where it could be seen through charred cloth was red and badly blistered. Unpleasant to look at, but not as bad as it could have been. There was no blackening, no cracking.

I dropped to the ground beside her, and got my ear close to her mouth. I didn't want to touch her if I could help it. I listened hard, filtered out the distant sound of traffic, and the summer country noises of birds and bugs.

I held my breath, and after a few seconds, I heard her breath, a little raspy, but strong.

"Jesus H. Christ!" Bates announced in a aggrieved tone. "What happened to you now?"

I sat up. "Nothing," I said. "Did you get through?"

"Yeah, they're on their way. I took the liberty of asking for the fire department, too. Some stuff in there is smoldering pretty good. Maybe we ought to move her away from the house."

"With the blast and the fall and all, I don't know about internal injuries. We'll move her if we see flames."

"Okay by me," he said. He looked down at her and drew in air through his teeth. "Poor woman, I just don't want her to get burnt any more. She's about done on this side, ain't she?"

"I hear sirens," I said. "Let the ambulance guys move her. They'll know what they're doing."

Which they did. Very efficiently, they started treating

Vivian Pike for burns and shock, got her onto a stretcher (still face down), and got her off to the hospital I'd visited the other day.

Just before they drove away, one of the attendants handed me my suit jacket and told me to hang around, the fire marshals would want to talk to me.

By this time the fire department had arrived. They showed up in a lime green pumper. Instead of thinking of anything of substance, which I was too agitated to do at the moment anyway, I decided to resent the truck.

The driver of the truck was a crew-cut, clear-eyed, middle-aged guy who looked a little like Clint Eastwood.

"Why green?" I demanded. "I mean, why *lime green?*"

"Huh?"

"Whatever happened to good old-fashioned fire-engine red?"

The driver looked bored. The smoldering had been taken care of, and the rest of the crew was winding up hoses.

"Tests have shown," he said, sounding as if he were quoting from an official report, which he probably was, "that this particular color offers the greatest visibility over the widest spectrum of lighting conditions."

"Come on," I said. "The thing is the size of a two-room bungalow. In comes down the road honking a horn like the roar of a brontosaurus, flashing red and white lights and blowing a siren. You mean to tell me that there has actually been somebody who has *failed* to see a fire truck?"

"I just drive 'em," Clint told me. "I don't buy 'em."

That was fair enough, but it also ended the conversation. I examined my jacket for a while. It smelled of burning hair, either because the wool had gotten scorched (which it had) or because it had soaked up the smell from Vivian Pike's burning blond tresses. It occurred to me that it smelled an awful lot like Rivetz's description of burning powdered rhino horn.

Absentmindedly, I started brushing the thing off with my hand, even though it was obvious that it was a total loss. I doubted that my renter's insurance would cover it. After all, I had deliberately slapped the thing on the fire myself.

My brushing hand struck something hard in the jacket pocket. I reached in and pulled out a black plastic rectangle and started to laugh.

Bates watched me balefully. He seemed to be taking this a lot harder than he'd taken the murder of his erstwhile houseguest.

"What's so funny," he demanded, "about a cellular phone?"

"Well for one thing," I said, "if I'd remembered it, I never would have sent you into the building, and we wouldn't have known about the danger of fire inside until this place was a pile of ashes."

He grunted.

"Another thing," I went on, "is that I'm glad I didn't beat her to death with the damned thing while I was putting the flames out."

"Yep," he said. "You're going to have enough trouble explaining this to the cops as it is, ain't you?"

"Am I?"

"You are if that was a bomb that got her. It was a bomb, wasn't it?"

"It was a bomb, all right." But that wasn't the half of it.

"... And away goes trouble,
down the drain."
—ROTO-ROOTER COMMERCIAL

17

Many, many, hours later, well into the dark hours
of Tuesday night, not far from the daylight of Wednesday
morning, I sat with Lieutenant Martin and Rivetz in an
all-night diner on Sixth Avenue and Thirteenth Street
called "Earnie's." With an "a."

I was hot, tired, grubby, frustrated, miserable, and stow-
ing away a dish of greasy hash and home fries that I did
not want. I was eating them, and washing them down with
some black acid calling itself coffee, because I was hoping
that heartburn would keep me awake.

It had been a busy day. The bomb had definitely been
the climax, but things kept hopping after that.

First of all, I was taken away by a fire marshal named

Smedley and some Very Angry Indeed local cops, who collectively wanted to know what the hell. I think the idea was what the hell the Network, as personified by me, was doing with guns and bombs in their peaceful burg, to say nothing of planting celebrities on them who exploit endangered species and then get themselves murdered across the state line so noisily that the echoes of the case hurt their eardrums.

Or something.

Whatever the hell they wanted to know, I really wasn't able to give it to them yet. I would have given them a lot to know what the hell myself.

As it was, all I could do was stick to the facts, although I must admit, after the ninth or tenth time through them, I was tempted to embroider them a little bit, just to see if they'd been paying attention.

After a few hours, the cavalry arrived in the form of Lieutenant Martin and Detective Rivetz. They had taken me into custody at the insistence of the Darien chief of police, who refused to let me run around the state of Connecticut a free man.

"Hey," I said, looking up from my plate. "Am I still in custody?"

Lieutenant Martin answered without taking his eyes off the bulldog edition of *Newsday*. "Yes. Now shut up and eat, or I'll put you in a cell."

I ate. Except for the coffee, it was pretty good stuff, I just wasn't in the mood for it.

I hadn't been in the mood for the hospital again, either, but that had been our next stop. There we got the good news that Vivian Pike was in no danger, that she wouldn't be scarred, at least not much, and that once her hair grew back, nobody'd even know she'd been blown up. Except herself, of course.

It would have been a different story if she'd still been

holding the envelope when the bomb when off. According to the fire marshal, in the unlikely event Vivian had lived, it would have been without a face or hands.

The doctors let us talk to her for a few minutes between the time she regained consciousness and the time she drifted off again to a Demerol-induced slumber.

I asked her what she'd wanted me for, when she'd come to the door and called my name. In a buzzing, sleepy voice she replied that there was a wire holding the top of the envelope, and she'd heard a click when she'd pulled it loose. The click had made her nervous, so she'd put the envelope down and gone to consult me about it.

She gave a feeble laugh. "Next time," she said, "I'll come clean down the stairs." She laughed again, then the laugh died away into a soft snore.

A doctor who looked about eleven years old said, "She's out. That's it. Maybe tomorrow, folks."

Cops don't ordinarily like getting chased, by doctors or anybody else, but Mr. M and Rivetz took it meekly this time, a mark, I thought, of the fact that they were as confused as I was.

This was a good trick, by the way, because I knew something—two things actually—they didn't know that made this case an even worse mess than it was. I was waiting for the proper moment to tell them.

Meanwhile, we stepped out of the treatment room into the waiting room to discover a scene that was positively surreal. Clem Bates was there, good as gold, sitting right where we'd left him, only now, sitting next to him and holding his hand with her unbandaged one was Barbara Bentyne Anapole.

She saw and us and gave us a warm smile. "Mr. Martin," she said. "Mr. Cobb. Mr. Rivetz." She gave Bates a reassuring pat, and disengaged. She stood up and came to us.

"I'm so glad to get a chance to see you all again." She

flushed. "I mean, I'm sorry that it has to be another occasion like this—this is a terrible thing, a terrible thing."

I was still caught too flatfooted by her appearance there to do anything but agree that it was indeed an absolutely terrible thing.

"What I should have said," she went on, "was that I'm happy for an opportunity to apologize for my behavior yesterday. I was in shock; I wasn't myself. I must have seemed quite hysterical, but I'm better now."

I raised an eyebrow. "You mean you realize . . ."

"Yes," she said. She was very serious. "I'm over my delusion now. I realize that my son Richard is dead."

"Oh," I said. Well, I thought, one delusion down and one big one left to go.

"That's why I'm here today, you see."

"Not exactly," I admitted.

"Why, because of poor Vivian. Who knows better than I do what she's going through? The shock of loss hasn't even had time to fully affect her yet, and then this terrible thing happens."

"How did you hear about it?" I asked.

She seemed surprised at the question. "On the radio. And just like yesterday, I caught the first train."

I turned to Lieutenant Martin. "Somebody in the Darien Fire Department has a big mouth."

Rivetz shook his head. "Emergency band radios. Every two-bit radio station and weekly newspaper in the country has got one, these days. I'm surprised at you, big TV guy and you don't know that."

"I knew it," I told him. "I just forgot."

Mrs. Anapole was sympathetic. "It's hard to remember things sometimes. Especially in times of stress. That's why I knew I had to be here for Vivian. We had our differences, and I don't know that I'll ever get over her trying to keep me away from my son, but I've come to accept the fact that she and I are the two people who loved Richard most, and who he most loved. We'll need each other in the days ahead, don't you agree?"

Mrs. Anapole took silence for assent and said she knew she was doing the right thing. "And your Mr. Bates has been so encouraging, too."

I would have given my Mr. Bates a swift kick in the ass about then, if I'd thought it would do any good.

I told Mrs. Anapole she had a good heart, which she did—it was her brain that was the problem. Then I excused myself, found the doctor, and warned him of the impending collision. He said he'd taken care of it; I told him I was glad it was his problem and not mine.

Next, I went back to the waiting room, grabbed Mr. Bates, and told the cops I'd meet them back in the city if they wanted to grill me.

"I'd like to grill you," Martin said, "like a chop. Why don't you and the Network haul ass off to New Jersey the way you're always threatening to do?"

From this, I gathered he was not in a good mood. I told them I'd drop by headquarters right after I delivered Mr. Bates and returned the Network car.

Bates wasn't too excited about the idea of being delivered. To him, remember, the purpose of this trip had been to allow him to breathe semi-country air and to relieve his boredom, and from that standpoint, it had been a big success.

"Why don't you keep me with you?" he suggested. "You might need someone to make another phone call."

"Oh yeah, you're a big help. Mrs. Anapole needs encouragement in her delusions the way I need another navel."

"Everybody has a right to try to arrange reality the way they want," he said, somewhat surprisingly. "That's what I've done," he said. "Mrs. Anapole does it with a little more imagination than most, that's all. What else does the pursuit of happiness mean, Cobb?"

"This is a pearl of homespun philosophy? The kind you were going to drop on the Bentyne show?"

"That's right. And don't think the country wouldn't be better off for hearing it, either."

I was delighted to drop him off at the Hilton.

"You'd better not leave me here to rot," he told me in parting.

I told him I'd arrange for the manager of the hotel to keep him in the freezer so he'd stay fresh. Then I drove the New York one-way street system for nine blocks in order to get one block south to the Network garage to drop off the car. I was delighted to do that, too. Sometimes I like driving, but lately it seemed every time I got behind the wheel, I wound up heading north like a duck in spring-time, splashing down at that goddamn house the Network bought, and up to my knees in ever-rising insanity.

Not that I was out of it yet. Having delivered the car, it was more or less incumbent on me to bring Falzet up to date. Not that I usually report to the Network president every time I step back in out of the rain, but Falzet had a personal interest in this one, and had made his desire to be kept up to speed on this matter manifest.

Tough, I thought.

I was in no mood for him, especially considering that there was something ahead I just couldn't avoid doing—I had to go talk to Lieutenant Martin before he got the idea I wasn't cooperating.

I flagged a taxi and let him do the driving. I told him whatever he did, not to turn north.

When I walked into headquarters that evening, the guy at the desk didn't even ask my name. He just handed me a visitor's badge and handed me the clipboarded sheets to sign.

It occurred to me that this was another place where I was spending too much time.

The lieutenant and Rivetz were both reading reports when I walked in. They kept reading them a good ten seconds before they looked up and greeted me.

Rivetz met my eyes first, pretended to be surprised.

"Whaddaya know," he said. "He meant it."

The lieutenant played along. "We're honored by your presence, O Media One."

"It occurred to me that you guys haven't actually questioned me, yet."

"New policy," Martin announced.

"Yeah," Rivetz said. "It never does any good to question you anyway. You tell us what you want, cover up what you want. All in an effort to keep your girlfriend rich."

Lieutenant Martin pushed down his springy white hair. "So from now on, I've decided not to waste the effort questioning you. I'm just gonna let you come across in your own good time."

"Gee," I said. "Perfect timing. Because I've walked in here bursting with things to tell you?"

"Oh yeah? What for instance?"

I laughed. "That policy lasted a long time, didn't it?"

The lieutenant made a couple of rude suggestions.

"No thanks," I said. "But you guys seem to be in a surprisingly good mood. Has there been some sort of break?"

"In the case? No, the case is as screwed up as ever. It's just that my depression muscles wore out. I also decided to keep my eyes focused straight ahead, and not worry about the razzle-dazzle you TV people throw off like sweat."

"What's that supposed to mean?"

"It means these nutty little sideshows that show up upon the fringes of the case. Your mountain man with his gun, shooting at shadows. The mother who isn't. All that crap. It isn't that stuff that's worrying me. Richard Bentyne is dead from poison. When I find somebody with the motive, opportunity, and means to have killed Richard Bentyne, I'm going to arrest that person, and only *then* will I worry about this fringe shit."

"I don't know," I said. "This is a fringe-time murder."

"What's that supposed to mean?"

"Any time between late local news and the Rise and Shine shows is called fringe time. It's the last frontier of expanding profits for the traditional TV networks. We paid Bentyne to make us a fortune on the fringes of the broadcast day."

"So?"

"So, maybe on a fringe-time murder, it's the stuff on the fringes that carries the real importance."

"You," the lieutenant said, "are simply trying to bust my ass and shake my confidence."

I grinned at him. "Maybe," I conceded.

"It won't work."

"Good for you. So, you've got the lift of a firm resolve. How about you, Rivetz?"

"What about me?"

"You seem more your old hostile self. Are you borne along on the lieutenant's tide, or do you think you see daylight somewhere?"

"I see daylight somewhere, but not in the case. My wife's gonna have the operation she needs."

"Hey, that's great!"

"Yeah. The doc said she hasn't waited too long, thank God, so her chance of coming through healthy is really good."

"What made her change her mind?"

"I did. I got fed up and yelled at her last night. I told her if she was so scared of the goddamn operation that she'd rather die than have it, that was her business, but she had some brass-bound nerve to say she was avoiding it because she wanted to be fair to *me*. I told her I did not love her for her tits, and that I didn't marry her for her tits. I told her I loved her for what she was inside, not outside, and if she didn't know that and believe it by now, our whole marriage was a joke, so she might as well forget being 'fair to me' and have the operation anyway."

"Wow," I said.

"Yeah. Anybody else ever talked to her like that, I'd a slugged him. As it was, I wanted to slug myself.

"But it worked. Before I knew it, she was in my lap like we were newlyweds, crying all over my paper and saying it was the nicest thing that ever happened to her.

"So, not being a dope, I called the doctor before she could change her mind."

"I'm glad it worked out."

"Yeah, me too. Now enough of the sentimental bullshit, tell the lieutenant what you're bursting to tell us."

"Sure," I said. "I'll tell you. But the first thing is only what you would call a fringe issue, so don't be disappointed."

"Yeah?"

"The reason Vivian Pike wanted me out there today was to tell me she was the one who gave Bentyne the rhino powder."

Fringe issue or not, they wanted to know all about it, so I told them. I included Marcie's having told me that Bentyne had actually been using the stuff for months before he was killed.

"Great!" Rivetz said. "Now we can forget all about the crap. It can't possibly have anything to do with his murder."

"Not so great," the lieutenant countered. "Once this gets out, there goes our smoke screen with the press, and they'll zero right back in on us again."

"There's no rule you have to tell the press, is there? I sort of promised Vivian Pike I'd keep her involvement quiet, if I could."

"Her story is still going to have to be checked. We'll tell

the L.A. cops to tiptoe, but you can't investigate a news operation without running into journalists, know what I mean?"

"I know. Just do the best you can."

"We will. Now what about the other thing you're so eager to tell us?"

"That envelope she opened—the one with the bomb in it."

"What about it?"

"The lab looking at it?"

"In Connecticut. They wouldn't let go of it. Them, I should say. It was torn up into a few pieces, as you might expect."

"Do they think they'll be able to read it?"

"They sounded optimistic. They can do some amazing things with damaged documents these days. They're supposed to call me when they're done. That's one reason we're hanging around the office, Why?"

"Because I got a good look at the letter. I saw the address."

"So?"

"It was addressed to Richard Bentyne. Not to Vivian Pike. Richard Bentyne."

"And you waited till now to tell us this?"

"I wanted to get rid of Bates first. I knew you'd want to talk about it."

The lieutenant grumbled but eventually accepted my reason for delay. That was nice, because it was a lie. The real reason was that I wanted some time to think about it myself.

"This raises a few possibilities," Rivetz said. "Did she open his mail as a regular thing? You think the guy who poisoned Bentyne was after a clean sweep?"

"The impression I got was that she didn't ordinarily open his mail. In fact, she looked at the envelopes, saw that it was all for him, and put it aside. I think she only opened the package, one, because it *was* a package—I don't know about you guys, but I'm always more curious about merchandise than I am about regular letters."

"I'm most curious about brown envelopes from the IRS," the lieutenant said.

Rivetz snorted. "I'd rather get a bomb."

"The other reason was that she was agitated, and wanted something to do with her hands. I don't think anybody could be sure she'd open that package."

"There's one way," Rivetz pointed out. "If she sent it herself. Shunt suspicion aside."

Rivetz, it blew her up. It could have killed her."

"She wasn't actually hurt bad, was she?"

"She isn't under much suspicion, is she?" I countered.

Lieutenant Martin intoned, "The wicked flee where no man pursueth."

"Yeah," I said, "but only the moronic playeth footsie with bombs for effect."

Rivetz grinned. "Not bad. I never believed it, anyway. But it happened in a mystery novel I read once."

"*The Dain Curse*, by Dashiell Hammett. Hammett himself said it was silly."

"Just something else we have to check," the lieutenant said. He leaned back in his chair. He had shifted into his wise-old-man-seen-it-all-done-it-all mode. He only did that when he was tried.

"But look," Rivetz said, "it still could have been intended to get the Pike woman. Bentyne was dead—somebody was bound to open the damn thing eventually."

"Not necessarily Pike, though," I pointed out. "She's not next of kin or anything, she was just shacking up with the guy. That bomb was just as likely to get Bentyne's mother—his real one, out West—or a lawyer as it was to get Vivian Pike."

Rivetz shrugged. "Well, a lawyer, what the hell? And as for the mother, this is a murderer we're talking about.

They're not known for sentimentality. Maybe it was worth a chance."

"Maybe," I said, "but what I'd like to see is the postmark on that envelope."

"What do you mean?"

"Well, I know it seems like forever, but Bentyne bit the big chicken on Monday morning—only yesterday. Which reminds me—if our killer was out to make a clean sweep, why didn't he poison Vivian Pike's coffee and Danish while he was at it?"

The lieutenant was professorial. "You're digressing, Matty. Keep to the point. Bentyne was killed late yesterday morning, early yesterday afternoon. What of it?"

"Well, it's not unknown for a letter to get from New York to Connecticut in a single day, but if that thing was mailed before yesterday, it means Bentyne was poisoned while another murder plan was already in the works."

The lieutenant's eyes opened wide. "And if it was mailed yesterday, or after say, noon yesterday . . ."

"Right. Somebody mailed him a bomb when he was already dead."

"Either way it doesn't make any sense, unless Rivetz is right. About the killer trying for the woman, I mean."

"I think," I said, "you ought to have a talk with the post office."

Which he did. He worked his way through various layers of federal employees until he reached someone both willing and capable of telling him what he wanted to know.

"All right," the lieutenant said, hanging up the phone. "This comes with no guarantees, but given traffic, volume of mail yesterday, and general procedures, he says the thing could have been mailed as late as one o'clock P.M. yesterday and made it to Darien, Connecticut, today—if it was dropped at the post office."

"Damn progress, anyhow," Rivetz said. "In the old days, the postmark, if we get it, would tell us exactly what time and what post office. Now it'll only have the date and 'New York' on it."

So now, all there was to do was wait. We waited for L.A. to come through on the rhino horn story, which they did about ten o'clock our time. And we waited and waited for the Connecticut lab to give us the word on the envelope fragments.

About four o'clock, the lieutenant hauled us out to Earnie's, insisting that grease was good for us.

Ten minutes to five, a warm glow had set up in my esophagus that would keep me awake for hours. The phone rang behind the counter, and a guy with tattoos virtually hidden by arm hair, possibly Earnie himself, said, "Lieutenant? It's your office. Connecticut's about ready to fax you something. That mean anything to you?"

We threw money at him and ran.

"You're in the picture!"
—JOHNNY OLSEN
You're in the Picture, CBS

18

It wouldn't do for us to wait until the fax came through, and then look at it like sensible adults. No. We had to cram into a closet with a civilian fax machine operator like clowns in a circus car, and watch it come across inch by inch.

"Why's it so dark?" I asked.

"They're sending a negative and a positive," the technician said. "Sometimes things show up one way better than the other."

So I stood there, sweating like an idiot, watching first a dark gray rectangle with some lighter gray on it appear, followed by a light gray rectangle with some darker areas.

When they'd both come through, along with some technical notes from Connecticut lab boys, the lieutenant grabbed them greedily and brought them back to his office. He lay the documents down on his desk and took a magnifying glass to it.

"There it is," he said. "17 Aug. Yesterday's date all right."

"A.M.," I added. "So it was mailed in the morning before Bentyne was killed, or almost literally before the body hit the floor. There's something funny about this?"

Rivetz was indulging himself in a fiendish chortle. "Post Office stuff. Federal business. I was just wondering how the blue boys were going to like this case."

"Of course, there's one possibility we didn't mention," I said.

"What's that?"

"Two different murderers."

The two cops groaned.

"We haven't mentioned it, Matty, because we don't want to think about it. If there's two of them out, there, we've got to catch them both, or there's no sense of catching any."

"Why?" I demanded.

"Because defense lawyers aren't stupid. 'You mean to say, Lieutenant, that though you accuse my client of poisoning Richard Bentyne, you have *no explanation whatever* for the bomb that exploded in his house that same morning. That by some *extraordinary coincidence* someone totally unknown to you was trying to murder Mr. Bentyne? Yet you deny the reasonable possibility that this person might have been responsible for the poisoning as well? *Really*, Lieutenant.' And on and on."

"I hate those guys," Rivetz said.

"It was the next day," I said.

"Huh?"

"The bomb went off the next day, not the same day. But you've made your point."

"Two killers is a nightmare. Even one killer and one

potential killer." The lieutenant shook his head. "Two cases to make. Two lawyers. Two trials. If, as I said, you catch them both in the first place. Enough to drive a cop to drink."

"Okay, okay. I'm sorry I mentioned it."

"All right, then. If, God forbid, it turns out to be true, we'll find out the bad news soon enough." Lieutenant Martin stretched and yawned. "Now, Matty," he said. "You got any other reason to be here?"

"You trying to get rid of me?"

"Hah!" he said. "I'm trying to get rid of *me!* I personally got five dozen reasons to hang around here, most of them in the form of paperwork."

"Me, too," Rivetz said.

"But paperwork doesn't do anybody any good when you're so tired it comes out alphabet soup. I'm gonna go home and get some sleep before I lose the knack."

"Me, too," Rivetz said.

"I've got to get home and walk the dog," I said.

Rivetz grinned. "Have fun. Don't break the poop-scoop law."

"Neither Spot nor I would dream of it. Good night."

The lieutenant massaged the back of his neck. "Yeah, good morning. Let us know if you get any more bright ideas, but not for, oh, twelve to sixteen hours, okay? After I wake up, I'm gonna want to eat."

I told I'm never felt farther from a bright idea in my life, started for the door.

"Matty?"

I turned. "What?"

"Nice haircut," the lieutenant said.

I walked and fed Spot, caught a few hours of sleep, a shower and a shave, and was at my desk at the Tower of Babble at a time not too unbecoming an executive of my stature. What I would have liked to have been doing was pounding my ear for another eight or ten hours, but I spent so little time actually at the office lately, I thought I'd better put in something longer than a cameo. We run a reasonably loose ship at Special Projects, but I didn't want Those Higher Up to start asking questions, either. Not that I didn't have the answers, mind you, I just didn't want the bother.

It was almost a relief to face a deskful of routine reports and queries.

Shirley Arnstein reported from Washington that it was in fact true that News's new Supreme Court correspondent was a Scientologist. Did we care?

As a strict believer in the First Amendment, I certainly didn't give a damn, as long as the guy didn't try to put the Chief Justice on the cans and discover his hidden traumatic birth engrams, which he wouldn't be able to do and keep his job, anyway. I decided to kick the whole matter back to News, with a recommendation that the Network mind its own damn business, and who over there started this inquiry, anyhow?

There was a short report from Harris Brophy. Harris's reports of failure were always short. In this case, he was telling me that nobody'd heard from Frank Harlan in a year and a half at least, but that he'd keep trying.

Well, I thought, Harris is the best there is. If he can't find Frank Harlan, then Frank Harlan was nowhere around to be found.

Who the hell was Frank Harlan?

It took me a good two minutes to remember. Frank Harlan was the writer who'd wanted to do the bio of Clement Bates. I'd wanted to talk to him, but the case had sort of twisted away from that line of thinking. I made a note to tell Harris to forget it, when I saw him.

Bookkeeping had sent a query—our expenses for June and July had been down 30 percent from the same period in the previous year—was there something wrong?

There is no pleasing these people. If you spend more than they think you should, they gripe about it, and if you spend less, like a true corporate hero, their sleazy little bookkeeping brains give birth to the suspicions that you're not doing your job.

I had Jazz get them on the phone, and once I had them, I explained with all the patience I could muster on three hours' sleep that Special Projects wasn't *like* other departments at the Network. We couldn't predict, we had to react. The reason we spent more money last June and July than for the same two months this year was that last year we had three potential scandals we had to defuse with a lot of travel and large-scale bribery, and this year we didn't.

The talk did about as much good as usual.

Then there was a note from Bart Eggelstein in Programming.

I thought, Programming? Programming was a bunch of people who sat in the dark all day long looking alternately at pilots of TV shows and computer printouts of demographics, arranging little blocks of time on a magnetic board, and giving themselves ulcers trying to figure out in advance what The American Viewer (whoever that was) was going to want to watch next season. They were kings and queens when they guessed right, and unemployed when they guessed wrong.

But isolated as they were, they never had anything to do with Special Projects.

The novelty of the thing led me to place the call to Bart Eggelstein myself. That and Network protocol. He and I were both vice presidents, but that's a lot like saying Carl Lewis and your golf-playing Uncle Wally are both athletes. Strictly true, but laughable in reality.

I got through to him in about a minute and a half, a pretty fair indication of our relative importance in the Network scheme of things.

"Cobb!" Eggelstein yelled. He wasn't mad, that was

just his style, a very New York style. He didn't just talk, he made declarations! The late Isaac Asimov was the same way. I think the fact that you usually find this trait in successful people is no accident—they always sound so excited about everything, you get swept along just talking to them.

"Yes, I'm returning your call."

"Yes! Very good of you to be so prompt!"

"What can I do for you?"

"Well, first of all, you could tell me what to put on in place of Bentyne. I'm going with old cop show reruns, but I don't like it. Also, I have an opening in my department, and I—"

There is a God, I thought. "I accept," I told him.

"You accept what?"

"Weren't you offering me a job in Programming?" Programing, I thought, where conflicts were measured in terms of share points, not bombs. Where I could work at the Network and actually do TV *stuff*, instead of being a sort of Private Eye on a leash. Programming, where for most of the year the hours were regular, and the biggest danger was an ulcer. I had never before perceived in myself such a burning desire to work there.

"No, I wasn't offering you a job! What kind of a job would I be able to offer you? You're already a vice president! The only job in my department it would be seemly for you to take would be my own!"

He paused for a second, the added as an aftershout, "And I'm not giving it up, yet!"

"I wouldn't want your job, Bart. For one thing, I'm not qualified for it."

"Let me tell you a secret: no one is qualified for this job! This job rewards the Lucky Guess and very little else!"

"So I take it you've already got somebody to file papers and sharpen pencils."

"Cobb! What's the matter? You sound unhappy!"

"No," I said. "Just tired."

"Ahh," he said, softly for him. "I know that feeling. But listen!"

I jumped.

"I do have a job here that I'm trying to fill. Assistant to the head of Daytime, insufficiently exalted for the likes of you!"

"And?"

"And one of the applicants has given you as a reference, which I am now checking."

"Oh? Who is it?"

"A Ms. Marcie Nast."

I laughed so loud I scared Bart, who ought to have been used to loud noises, living as he did in daily proximity to his own voice.

It was at least a minute before I could get an intelligible word out of my mouth.

"Bart," I breathed, "I'm sorry."

"It's okay! Only I'd like to be in on the joke!"

If it was a joke on anybody, it was on me. "Listen!" I said. I was beginning to sound like him. "She gave me as a reference knowing exactly what I was going to say, and I'll bet she figured it would help her get the job, at that."

Either that, I thought, or she was counting on my remembering how ready she was to fling sex-discrimination and harassment charges around, and come through with a glowing little ginger cake endorsement. If that was the case, she was reading from the wrong volume.

But it didn't sound like her. All she wanted was to put her size seven-and-a-half foot on the next step up the ladder. But if someone telling the truth about her could help her get a shapely leg on the next rung, she was perfectly willing to accept the truth. Hadn't she told me she was always perfectly frank when it didn't make any difference?

"Well?" Bart Eggelstein demanded. "What *are* you going to say? By now, I am positively dying to hear it!"

"In my opinion," I said, "Marcie West is an acculturated psychopath. I think she is totally ambitious and totally ruthless. Think? She told me so, in so many words. If there are any women in your department between her and the top, she'll do anything she can to discredit them. Men, too, possibly. If you'll excuse a personal question, you're pretty close to retirement age, aren't you?"

"Three years."

"Then you're probably safe."

"And she gave you as a reference?"

"I'm not finished. From what I've seen of her, if you put her in a position where she's convinced the best way ahead for her is to do the best possible job for you, she'll do the best job you ever saw. She could do a historically good job. On drive alone. Just don't trust her farther than you could throw a steamroller."

"Mmmmm," Bart said, then was silent for a minute. "How long have you known this young lady?"

"Two days."

"She makes a big impression, doesn't she?"

"If she wants to."

"Would you hire her?"

"If this were a war, and I was in the OSS, I'd hire her in a shot. Under the current circumstances—well, I could possibly handle her, but I'll just say I'm glad I don't have any openings."

"Ambition and ruthlessness, I don't have to tell you, are not necessarily undesirable qualities in a TV executive!"

"They certainly help get things done—if getting things done is all you care about."

"People in this department have been in a rut . . . It might be a good idea to light a fire under them . . ."

"I think it would be more like throwing an M-80 in the middle of them."

"What's an M-80?"

"Firecracker," I said. "A big one. Equal to a quarter stick of dynamite."

"All the better! Get people jumping around here! You know, Cobb, I'm three years away from retirement, and already the power plays around here you wouldn't believe. A joker in the deck might prove very interesting. Could liven up my declining years considerably."

I laughed again, a soft chuckle this time. "So you're going to do it?"

"I think I will! Yes, I will! Her ambition and ruthlessness will make us supreme in the ratings into the next century! Or not! Either way, if what you say is true, she'll open a few eyes around here!"

"She'll do that, all right. Bart, do me a favor, will you?"

"What's that?"

"Let me know once you tell her she's got the job. I think I want to talk to her."

I *did?* I hadn't realized it until the words were out of my mouth.

"I'll do better than that. I'm calling her right away. Wait ten minutes, then ring her. She's at her brother's shop."

I spent the ten minutes wondering what the hell I thought I was doing, but at the end of it, I made the call.

"It's been real."
—Ernie Kovacs
The Ernie Kovacs Show, CBS

19

But the suddenly very busy Assistant to the Director of Daytime wouldn't talk to me on the phone. I could, however, allow her to take me to dinner tonight, by way of celebration.

"I don't think—"

"We could discuss baseball strategy," she said.

"I still don't—"

"Or I could tell you what I've remembered about Poor Richard's death. It could be something you ought to know."

"Yeah? Suppose I just arrange for the cops to meet you for dinner? They know a great place for home-fried potatoes. Then you can tell them directly."

"But, Matt dear, I don't want to tell *them,* I want to tell *you.* You're much more amusing than they are."

"But what if the cops kind of show up, anyway?"

"Don't be tiresome. I'll just tell them I made it all up in attempt to get you to go to dinner with me."

"One of these days," I told her, "you're going to run out of these fast answers."

"I doubt it," she said breezily. "But wouldn't it be fun for you to be around if I do?"

I didn't answer. She went on. "Shall we say sixish? Do you want to *eat* eat, or just sit around, like last time?"

"You're paying? I want to eat."

"Oh, Matt, you definitely show promise. Do you know Mazzaroni's on Eighth Avenue, in the village?"

"I know it. Give me a chance to get downtown. Make it six-thirty, instead."

There are several kinds of Italian restaurants in the Village; in the whole city, really, but like in everything else, in Greenwich Village, they go to extremes. One extreme is the little mom-and-pop place, with ten tables in enough space for six, with red-and-white tablecloths, and the inescapable chianti bottles with candles stuck in them. You can get some incredible food in a place like this, especially pasta sauces, but you've got to try a bunch of them before you find one that suits you. These are no places to have private conversations, for all they're described as "intimate little places." What happens is, on a busy night, you get intimate with the owners, their kids, and the other nine couples in the restaurant.

At the other extreme are places that pretend to be outposts of the Roman Empire, and always have names like Caesar's Forum, forget the fact that no Caesar ever ate pasta or anything like it. Caesar's Forum will be spread out over three floors, be covered in flocked satin wallpaper in some shade of beige or pink, resemble a jungle in the number of potted plants inside it, and have a huge fountain in the middle surrounded by reproductions of antique statuary. Again, the food may be surprisingly good, but the waiter will wear a short-jacketed tuxedo and speak with an Italian accent. He will also refer to the woman as Madame, and never speak directly to her.

If the place in question happens to be in Brooklyn, and you eat there regularly, you've got a decent chance to see some Mafia guy get blown away every eighteen months or so. Of course, they come in clusters, so it's hard to tell.

It occurred to me that Marcie was just the type to enjoy seeing a well-staged rub-out, but I doubt she would ever go more than once to a place where the waiter never spoke to her directly.

She picked a good place. Mazzaroni's had enough room for a private talk, the food was great, and for decor, they had more food. I had a prosciutto secco the size of a truck tire hanging over my head at the corner table the waitress (who spoke pure New York) showed me to.

"Good to see you." Marcie smiled as I joined her.

"I'm hungry," I said. "Ready to order?"

"I've had a peek at the menu," she conceded.

"All right. I don't need the menu; I always get the same thing when I come here."

The waitress came by. Marcie ordered a house red, I went for San Pellegrino water. It was more expensive than seltzer, and she was paying. For appetizers, she ordered an antipasto, and I asked for prosciutto and melon.

The waitress made a face. "The melon is kind of hard, today," she said. It was another reason I liked this place.

"Oh, thanks. I'll have *prosciutto e crostini* instead." The waitress approved.

She also approved our main dish choices, *pasto con carne misto*, which was shell macaroni in a rich tomato sauce with hunks of beef, pork, and veal for Marcie, while I took *pollo fiorentino*, boned chicken breast in a thin egg batter cooked in butter over spinach, ditto.

The waitress read it back to us, then marched off with

the air of someone happy in her work. I grabbed a sesame seed breadstick, bit the end off it, and pointed the rest at Marcie.

"Now," I said. "You're going to tell me what you remembered, the thing my friends the cops would want so much to hear."

"I never said how *much* they'd want to hear it. I just said they'd want to."

"Stop stalling. Out with it."

"For God's sake, sit still long enough to finish your breadstick first. You could at least pretend you could stand to be with me."

"You, the high priestess of frankness, want me to pretend? Here's me being frank: it scares me, but I can stand to be with you. You're fascinating, the way a train wreck is fascinating. No, the way a snake is fascinating in nature films as it calmly goes about the business of swallowing a goat."

At that point, our appetizers arrived.

Marcie smiled. "Great timing, Matt." She took a huge forkful of lettuce and cheese and salami and lifted it to her mouth. She opened her pretty mouth wide, then suddenly wider, as though she'd unhinged her jaws. It was a remarkably snakelike illusion.

She put her fork down on her plate and laughed. "Oh, you sweet-talker, you."

"Very funny," I said. "But the core of the message is the same: you scare me. If the thing about the case was a scam, I'm walking out of here no matter how good the food is."

"No scam, Matt dear." She sighed. "Oh, all right, if you can talk about snakes swallowing goats while we eat, I suppose I can talk about poison while we eat."

"It's about poison?"

"I would suppose so. It's about the flypaper. One of

the log-cabin props, you remember. From Clement Bates."

"Yeah," I said. "I remember Clement Bates. He's my other unforgettable character from this case."

"Well," she said, "the police asked us an awful lot about flypaper, especially the angry little one with the hat."

"Rivetz," I said.

"I suppose so. Anyway, later they wanted especially to know about some missing sheets from the package. Because, I found out later, you can distill arsenic from flypaper, and of course arsenic is what killed Richard. I didn't know anything about the flypaper itself."

"But?" I prompted.

"But," she said, "one of the incredibly tedious jobs Vivian made me do was to check the parcels and packages as they came in—not to open them, just to look at addresses, shipping weight, things like that, in order to double check the people in the mailroom over at the Tower of Babble. Apparently she had some trouble with them in the first days of the show.

"Anyway, I remembered getting a parcel from Bates the week before the fateful day, a neat little rectangle, shipping weight sixteen and a half ounces. I logged it in with the rest. You can probably see the document in Vivian's office, if they haven't cleaned it out yet. How is she, by the way?"

"She'll be okay. Burned up and down her back, but nothing worse than second degree."

"I'll bet she wishes she still had someone going over her mail."

"Yeah, and I'll bet I know who that is." I remembered some of the other stuff the lieutenant had gotten from the lab before I'd left. It was a small-scale incendiary, easily made from everyday ingredients, and you could learn how to make one from at least six different books circulated at various revolutionary radical bookstores (yes, we still had them—the city is like a people zoo, we preserve endangered species long after they become extinct in the outside world) within blocks of police headquarters or this very restaurant.

This type of letter bomb was very popular with the IRA in the late seventies and early eighties. It produces a very small, but very intense fireball, and it's built with a sweet little delay switch that usually ensures the victim is either looking into the envelope, or actually holding the bomb in his hand when it goes off.

"I'm glad she's okay," Marcie said.

I looked at her.

"I mean it," Marcie said. "She's out of my way, and I'm out of her reach. She hates me now, but in a few years, I'll be in a position to throw a lot of work her way—she's a very good producer, you know—and then she'll love me."

"Tell me more about flypaper," I said.

"Matt, you can't sit there thinking I'm inhuman, and I know you do, then jump all over me when I inquired about the welfare of a fellow being."

"Flypaper."

"Oh, all right. Today I remembered how on Monday morning the cops showed us the package of flypaper, torn open at the corner, you know? And asked us about it. It occurred to me today that that's what might have been in the sixteen-and-a-half-ounce rectangular package.

"Luckily, I remembered the brand name—Pestik."

"Sounds like a linebacker for the Steelers," I said.

"I like the L.A. Raiders."

"Figures. What about Pestik?"

"I went looking for some. Hardware stores, you know. And I found some! Who would have thought you could find old-fashioned flypaper in Manhattan today? I found the identical package, and I had the man at the store weight it. It weighed sixteen ounces, exactly."

"So allow half an ounce for wrapping paper and tape, and there's your package."

"Not only that," she said. "Herbie, the prop man, had been sick and missed a few days, so the package stayed locked up in my cabinet until I gave it to him on Monday morning."

I sat up. "Is that solid?"

"Absolutely. Of course, I haven't proved *conclusively* that the flypaper was in that package, but it does sort of present itself, doesn't it?"

"It presents itself, all right," I said. "What, if anything, do you think you *have* proved?"

She thought it over, touching the tip of her tongue to the middle of her upper lip.

"Assuming that the package *did* contain the flypaper, I *think* I've proven that he wasn't poisoned with it. Doesn't it take more time to get the arsenic out of the paper than there was?"

I told her it did. I didn't tell her that the cops already *knew* it wasn't the flypaper but Deth-on-Ratz—they were saving that.

"It proves something else, too," I said. "Assuming, as always, that your parcel was the flypaper. And assuming you're telling the truth."

"Why should I be lying about this?"

"God knows."

"What else did I prove?"

I just grinned. Marcie was going to get insistent, but just then the waiter came with our main courses. It wasn't until the smell of butter and lemon and garlic hit my nostrils that I realized how hungry I was.

"*Buon appetito,*" I smiled, and dug in.

Marcie, of course, had no intention of letting it go at

that, but after three or four attempts, she finally accepted that the subject was closed.

Then we just talked. We talked about the food. We talked about baseball, as advertised. She said she was a great admirer of George Steinbrenner (I said that figured too) and weren't the Yankees doing great this year?

I enjoyed it, as I enjoyed dinner, but in the back of my mind was a nagging irritation caused by Marcie's little spell of detective work. Couldn't she see what else her story of the package indicated?

It indicated that on that fateful Monday morning, not only was poison being prepared for the famous Richard Bentyne; not only was a bomb being dropped in the mail addressed to same, it also meant somebody had been sneaking around the studio stealing flypaper for *no goddamn reason whatsoever.*

As with dumping the arsenic in the chicken itself, anybody could have snitched the flypaper, from Vivian Pike, who had conflicting motives and had been the victim of the bomb, to Marcie Nast, who had only the feeblest of motives and brought the matter to my attention (without her, who would have known?), to Millionaire Mountain Man Clement Bates, who not only had no motive whatsoever but was the *owner* of the wretched stuff in the first place.

Coincidences happen all the time; if you think about it the right way, everything that ever happens is coincidental to something. I could take a simultaneous bomb-mailing and poisoning. But this was too much, or rather, too many. I hated it, but that was nothing to the way Lieutenant Martin was going to react when he found out he suddenly had three perps to look for. Maybe. It might have been more merciful not to tell him, but of course I'd have to.

Since it could not possibly figure in the commission of Bentyne's murder itself, I decided to tell him tomorrow.

Let him enjoy the rest of the day. Maybe I could forget about it until the morning and enjoy the rest of mine, too. Roxanne was coming home tomorrow, and that would save the day no matter what else happened.

So I crammed it into a box and gave my full attention back to the remarkable specimen I was having dinner with.

Dessert came, zabaglione over strawberries.

"Welcome back," she said.

"I haven't gone anywhere. I've been talking to you. You were telling me that you'd think of a way to get our Thursday afternoon rating up if it killed you."

"Sure," she said. "Your ear-to-mouth circuit was hooked up, but your brain was long gone. Thinking about me, I hope."

"Not exactly."

She faked a sigh. "And I had such hopes." She patted her lips daintily with a napkin.

"Now, Matt," she said, "I can tell you why I wanted to have dinner with you."

"To get your information before the cops," I said. "So that if the case is ever solved and your information had anything to do with solving it, you could claim a slice of the credit. The publicity couldn't hurt a woman on her way to the top."

She tilted her head. "Well, there was that, too. But mostly, it was to say good-bye."

"Are you going somewhere? Or am I?"

"Not physically. We are both going out of each other's lives."

"God, you make it sound as if we're Siamese twins. Not only did I just meet you two days ago, I don't even like you."

She waved that away. "I've told you before, I could make you. That's not the point."

"What is the point?"

"The point is that you're dangerous for me to be around."

If you asked me, the only things she needed to be afraid of were crosses, wooden stakes, and silver bullets, but I let her go on.

"You bother me," she said. "I'm attracted to you physically, but anybody who can't control that is no better than an animal, don't you agree?"

"Go on."

She smiled. "You don't have to say it, Matt. I know you do. You make me crazy."

"How do I do that?"

"You've got the brains, the outlook, the attitude, and the talent to be truly *free*. Like me. I've never met anyone else like me, have I told that?"

"Neither have I."

"But you could be. I saw you in action. At the studio. At the softball game. You can cut loose, be the center of the universe. I've seen it, just for split seconds at a time, but I know it's there.

"And then when it's done, you voluntarily slip back into your chains. You could fly, Matt!"

"Like you."

"Yes, like me! You could soar. But instead you stagger along under the weight of lies like other people matter, or that there are standards outside yourself you need to live up to. It's sad to see an eagle with his wings clipped, but it's infuriating when he insists on clipping his own.

"Every time I see you, I think of what you might be, if you let yourself. Of what we could do together. We could take over the Network in two years, not the ten it's going to take me on my own. The Network? *Fuck* the Network! We could rule the whole city."

"Tomorrow the world," I suggested.

She thought about it, shook her head. "Too unwieldy. Besides, we need opposition, or we'd get bored."

Now I shook my head.

"But you see how you are? If you were like me, I could trust you, fully like me, I mean, because I would arrange things so your best selfish move would be to do what I wanted you to, and you'd treat me the same way, and we'd both prosper. But I'm not going to live forever, Matt, and there's a lot I want to do. I can't spend the time and energy training you out of bad habits. So, for my own sake—"

"Which is why you do anything."

"Which is the only intelligent reason ever to do anything, I am going to see to it that our paths never cross again."

"Suits me," I said. "As it will probably please you to know, I foresee your becoming a legend, a legend I'll undoubtedly be doing my part to spread. As for a more personal good-bye, it's hard to know what to say. It doesn't even do any good to feel sorry for you, because you have no way of even imagining the excitement and the glory of just being human. You'd treat sympathy with contempt."

Her dark eyes held mine. "Yes, I would."

"I won't even analyze the emotion in me that doesn't want your contempt. I'll just keep my mouth shut. Why don't you pay up—you did invite me, after all—and I'll put you in a cab?"

"I live nearby, just walk me home."

"Won't that fill your head with pictures of frustrated eagles?"

"I can stand it for five minutes. Or I can walk home alone."

"No. What you'd call my voluntary weakness makes me want to keep even you from getting mugged."

"And that," she said, "is why no one can stop me."

It was less than five minutes. We walked wordlessly to

a little apartment house on a deserted back street. You can find those, in Greenwich Village, even at eight o'clock at night.

She opened the downstairs door. "Good-bye Matt," she said.

I told her, "Fare thee well."

She smiled and gave me a last, soft lingering kiss that still felt warm on my lips after she'd stepped quickly inside and run upstairs.

"It's the Toast of the Town!"
—JULIA MEADE
Toast of the Town, CBS

20

I forgot about my lips when my ears started to tingle.

It wasn't that the footsteps behind me were so noisy, they weren't noisy at all, just barely perceptible. And they weren't the normal footsteps of someone in sneakers, either. These were muffled, all right, but also furtive, and the rhythm of them was wrong. They matched mine, faster when I walked faster, slower when I slowed down.

One set of footsteps, and that didn't make sense, either. At six two, maybe two hundred fifteen pounds (just about my basketball-playing weight), I am not typical New York mugger bait. They like easy pickings. If a lone mugger tries on someone like me, it usually means he's too strung out on drugs to pronounce surreptitious, let alone act that way.

I kept walking, listening hard. Did I hear another set of footsteps, some way farther off than these, or was I just imagining it?

I ran through the unwritten but universally followed New Yorker's survival manual. Turning on him (or her or them) might provoke an attack; on the other hand it might scare them off, particularly if I acted crazy enough loudly enough.

I decided to throw a look over my shoulder to check things out, then decide whether or not to scream. A good angry scream is always best in situations like this. My favorite move is to beat my fists together and yell, *"Are you ready?"* Since the potential mugger doesn't know what he's supposed to be ready for, he tends to decide I'm not worth the risk.

I waited until I was under a street lamp, so I'd have the best chance to size things up before I committed myself to an act of public lunacy.

I turned. He was the right size and shape to be a mugger, on the tall side of medium and wiry. He was also walking with his hands in his pockets, a good way to hide a switchblade or a gun.

I was all set to go into my psycho act when he spoke to me.

"Matt?"

He came farther into the circle of lamplight.

"Peter, for God's sake, I thought you were a mugger."

He was smiling when he caught up to me.

"Hi," he said. "I thought it was you, but I would have been embarrassed to call out if I'd been wrong, you know how that is. So I thought I'd catch up and pass, and then see if it was you."

I told him I did the same thing. "Gets a little spooky, though, on these quiet back streets."

"What brings you down this way? Visiting Marcie?"

"Just seeing her safely home. We had dinner together."

"Early night," he said.

"It wasn't a date or anything," I told him. "Marcie wanted to celebrate her new job."

"I know. She was speaking from Coif You!"

"That's right," I said. "I remember. Listen, speaking of that, I've gotten nothing but compliments on my haircut."

"Good to hear."

A ramification of the Marcie Declaration that had escaped me previously now sprang to mind.

"Listen, Peter," I said. "I'm sorry, but the softball team is going to have to get along without me."

"I know that, too."

He was still smiling, but the smile seemed to be slowly fading, like an old Polaroid snapshot that hadn't been dipped in the fixer. I wondered if he was okay.

I was about to ask him, when he took a sand-filled sock out of his pocket and coshed me in the side of the neck with it. He hit me two more times before I hit the pavement, on the left ear and on the top of the head. When I reached the concrete, he started kicking me.

I was dazed but not out. I still had enough sense and control of my body to roll up in a ball, but only that much. I certainly couldn't stand up and fight back; I could barely feel the sidewalk beneath me. All I could see were bright dancing colors just in front of my eyes, a new explosion of which went off with every kick. I tried to ask him why he was doing this, but I was too stunned to form words.

"Bastard," he said.

He stopped kicking me. My muscles untensed a little, involuntarily. Something wet and cold hit me. For a moment, I thought he was throwing water on me to revive me.

But it wasn't intended to revive me, and it wasn't water. My nose told me what it was—gasoline.

I had to get out there. I tried to struggle to my feet, but

I only succeeded in humping myself up a little bit, then rolling over sideways.

Peter laughed and followed me.

My eyes were starting to clear. I could see things, but they were smeary. My hand on the dirty pavement. Peter's face, smiling. The bright colors had gone away, all but one. The one that stayed was the white-red flame of the traffic flare Peter held in his hand.

"You're going to die, Matt," he said. He might have been telling me I was going to bat second. "They tell me it hurts."

I almost made it to my feet, but he coshed me again, hitting me across the left shoulder. I went down, and my arm went numb. This time, though, I found a friend. A nice, rough, brick wall. Planting my right hand against it, I finally made it to my feet.

"Congratulations," Peter said. "Not that it makes much difference. You'll burn as brightly standing as you would lying down."

He came closer, holding the flare up like some perverted Statue of Liberty.

The image of him rocked before my eyes. In the shape I was in, even standing with my back against a solid wall was like trying to stand in a rowboat in a hurricane.

I could see one chance, and I was going to try it. I was going to rush him, hoping to get in under the flare, but even if I didn't, to rush him and clamp my good arm around him and not let go no matter what. Then we could both taste hell together. He might even realize that burning me meant burning him, and drop the flare altogether.

If that happened, I swore to God, I would strangle Peter slowly.

I rocked back against the wall, pushing off with all the strength I could summon. I jumped for him.

I made a good start, too, but after the second step, my legs crumbled beneath me, and I wound up lunging weakly for Peter's knees. One step back and he was out of my reach again.

I was on the sidewalk at his feet, breathless, listening to him laugh. The gas was very cold, and was making me shiver. It would, I knew, be warming me up in a few moments.

Peter brought the flame closer. I put my arm up to shield my face, just as though I expected it to help. At least it blocked the sight of his grin.

I wanted to pray; I couldn't think of anything to say except please don't let this goddam maniac do this to me.

Then a voice said, "Peter."

Marcie's voice.

"I glanced out my window and saw you duck out of a doorway and follow Matt. What are you doing?"

"He's been messing around with you, sis. He doesn't love you, I can tell. The other one, didn't either, Bentyne. They just weren't good enough for my Marcie."

Marcie got closer to her brother. Her lovely face was impossible to read in the harsh red light of the flare.

"Peter?" she said softly. "Listen to me."

Peter shook his head. "He's got to die, sis. For your sake. I can't stand the thought of him pawing you, putting his filthy mouth on you. I stood it with Bentyne, because . . ." He paused as if he couldn't remember because of what. "Because you said you were using *him*."

"I was."

"I don't *care!*"

He sounded like a four-year-old on the verge of a tantrum.

"It's not right. You shouldn't have to let them abuse you like that just so you can get ahead at their stupid Network!

"And anyway, Matt couldn't do anything for your career. He's just another filthy, lecherous pig, and he's got to die."

"Of course he does," she said.

Her brother looked suspicious. "But *I've* got to be the one to do it," she said.

"You?"

"I'm the one he's victimized, after all."

"You shouldn't have to do this. You shouldn't even have to see it. It's going to be gruesome."

"He deserves it," she insisted. "Give me the flare," she said.

"No."

"Yes," she said. "Give it to me before it burns out."

"It's not *right.*"

"It's perfectly right. I have the right to burn him, because of what he is, and what he makes me feel inside."

Oh, Jesus, I thought.

"I'll burn him, Peter, I'll burn him right out of my life, him and all the rest of them. Then I'll settle down with the one and only man in the world who *is* good enough for me."

Peter scowled. "And who's that?"

"*You,* darling, you. You're my brother and my father and my only friend. You deserve to be my lover, too."

The flare backed away from me an inch, giving me room to take a shallow breath.

Peter was in tears.

"But we *can't!*" he wailed.

Marcie was right next to him now. "Shh, darling, shh. We'll talk about that part of it when we're done with this. Now give me the flare."

His voice could barely be heard over the hissing of the flame. "I love you, Marcie." He gave her the flare.

Immediately, she threw it out into the middle of the street, where it landed in a pothole, popped, hissed, sizzled, and went out.

Meanwhile, she was wading into him, slapping his face with loud resounding wallops.

"You stupid son of a bitch!" _(pow!)_ "Don't you know what something like this could do to my plans?" _(pow!)_ and so on.

Peter stood there and took it. I don't know how long it would have lasted if I hadn't gotten to my feet and delivered a pow myself that laid him out.

As I bent to relieve him of the final flare, Marcie said, "Well. At least this will get _him_ out of my hair."

"... And out in left field ..."
—Vin Scully
Major League Baseball, NBC

21

It seemed strange to be in a hospital without Lieutenant Cornelius U. Martin Jr., and Detective First Grade Horace A. Rivetz at my side, but I could excuse their absence. After I had phoned them from the emergency room of Bellevue Hospital, they had gone with all possible dispatch to first, the Sixth Precinct, in the Village, where the cops had custody of Peter Nast, hairdresser and arsonist, and second, to the premises of Coif You! and the apartment of Mr. Nast.

It seemed a little strange to be the patient, too. It is my belief that a hospital gown is the single greatest incentive to good health ever invented. Who are these things designed for, anorexic midgets?

I was, however, in too much pain to work up too big a

grump about it. I'd been washed and anointed (scraped my knees, crawling around), but had been given no pain-killers until the extent of my concussion could be assessed.

I'd told them to assess away, so they hooked me up to numerous machines, poked my head into something that looked like a miniature front-loading washer, shone lights in my eyes, and asked me trick questions.

I could have slept through most of it, except I'd been warned not to fall asleep.

So I thought about the case instead.

I wondered, first of all, if Peter had been a poisoner, a bomber, or in some arcane way we'd never know if he didn't explain, both.

I marveled how he'd never crossed my mind as a suspect. Blindness. New York decadence–induced blindness. So, she was sleeping with somebody, and her brother knew it, so what. Post–sexual revolution blindness. Who could believe that a brother would get so worked up over his sister's honor? I mean, even if he coveted it for himself?

I myself had teased the lieutenant about the would-be King of Fringe Time being killed by someone on the fringes of the case.

I'd delivered the warning, all right, then I'd gone right back into the rut of assuming that the Forty-Five-Million-Dollar Man had to be the victim of a Forty-Five-Million-Dollar Plot.

I made a noise. The medical technician wanted to know if I was all right. A doctor came and told me to squeeze his finger. I obliged.

There was no problem on that score. No further problem at least, aside from scrapes and scratches, a shoulder bruised to the bone, and God knows what rearrangements inside my head. That little yelp had come out because my brain still wouldn't let go of the money. There was something about the money, something important . . .

Then I got it. "Hah!" I said.

"Am I hurting you?" the technician wanted to know.

It's hard to talk when your skull feels like it's in the middle of the spin cycle, but I managed to tell him, no, I'd just thought of something.

It took another hour and a half, but finally, they wheeled me to a room, gave me a shot in the ass, which had been one of the few parts of my body that didn't hurt already, and told me that as far as their tests were concerned, if I went to sleep now, I almost certainly wouldn't die before I woke.

I decided to take them up on it. Whatever had been in the needle had taken all the pain away. I went to sleep.

I woke up looking into the big brown eyes of Roxanne Schick.

I grinned sleepily at her. "Hi, honey," I said.

Softly, she stroked my forehead. "I leave you alone for a little while, and look what happens to you. Are you all right, Cobb?"

"Getting there. I'll be sleeping on my left side for a while."

"You're sure, now."

"Positive."

"Good. So maybe now you feel up to telling me why this guy wanted to burn you to death for messing with his sister."

I started to laugh. It hurt, but I couldn't stop. I was gratified to see Rox was laughing, too.

"Hyperactive imagination," I said. "His I mean. Also, if you can stand my being psychological about it, he wanted to burn me to death because *he* wanted to mess with his sister."

"A wacko," Rox summarized.

"Your command of medical jargon is impressive."

"Shut up," she said pleasantly. After a few seconds, she

said, "Cobb, I don't want to find you in the hospital every time I turn my back on you for a minute. You've got to stop hanging around with murderers."

"I don't do it on purpose," I said.

"Well, cut it out." Suddenly, she dropped the banter, something she only did when we were alone, and not often then. "Matt, I lost my parents and most of my childhood. If I lose you, I don't think I'm going to make it."

"It comes up in the course of the job," I told her.

"Mmmm," she said. "Well, I *am* the major stockholder in the Network. Maybe I ought to pull a few strings and get you fired."

"Maybe you should," I said.

Her eyes opened wide.

"But not yet."

She tossed her head in disgust. "I should have known," she said.

"Look," I said, "I've got to cozy up to one more killer. Then this job will be finished and we can talk."

"You mean that?"

"Promise."

"I'll hold you to it."

I grinned at her. "You do that. There's a lot of things I want you to hold me to."

Roxanne spoke in her throat, mock-vampishly. "Oh, I will, Big Boy. I'll hold you *very* close, but tenderly, so as not to bend your bruises."

"I can hardly wait," I said.

I tried to sit up. I saw enough stars to have a new galaxy named after me, but with some help from my beloved, I finally made it.

"Do I have a phone in here?"

"What do you want a phone for?" Roxanne demanded. "I'm already here."

"Yes," I said. "God is good." I leaned out and kissed her, a maneuver easily worth the pain it caused. "Unfortunately," I went on, "what I need to do now is to speak to Lieutenant Martin."

"Oh," Roxanne said. "Forget the phone."

"What am I supposed to do?" I asked. "Stick my head out the window and yell?"

"That will not," she said haughtily, "be necessary. He's here."

"Where, here?"

She smiled. "My, you did get hit on the head, didn't you? You sound like a telegram."

"Where is he, Rox?"

"Down at the nurses' station. I've been sort of fending him off you."

"Well, go on down there and fend him on me, will you?"

"What a disgusting idea."

"Now, don't be politically incorrect," I said. Then, seriously, I added, "Come on, Rox, I need to talk to the man. It's about time we got this straightened out."

She gave me a soft kiss, bending no bruises, but making Marcie's efforts seem like soap bubbles by comparison. "Be right back," she said.

She was, too, but at least she had the lieutenant in tow. He looked me over.

"The thing about white people," he said, "is that they show bruises really badly."

I tried to adjust the wretched hospital gown to cover my shoulder.

"And their hair," he went on. "So untidy." He took off his hat to show his white crop. "Now, a nice head of nappy curls like mine stands up to sweat, beatings, women, and always looks nice and neat."

"Does the name Don King mean anything to you?"

"Nope," he said, "not a thing. You had us worried, Matty. How you doing?"

"Can't talk about it now, I'll be late for my rumba

lesson." I shrugged as well as I could with one shoulder. "What can I say? It hurts, I'm stiff. Doctor last night said they didn't think I was sick enough to continue taking up a bed."

"You'll go home," Roxanne said. "Spot will protect you. I'll take care of you."

"Sounds great," I said.

"I'll call a taxi," she volunteered.

"But not yet."

"Fooey."

I turned to the lieutenant. "You don't look like you've had much sleep."

"Ha," he said. "I spent the night with Mr. Peter Nast. With him, and supervising the search of his apartment."

"And?"

"What, and?"

"He gets it from you," Roxanne said.

"Gets what from me?"

"Never mind," I said. "I'll tell you. Peter is under arrest for attempted murder on me, and possibly attempted arson. You are also holding him jointly for the Connecticut cops and the Feds for attempted murder on Vivian Pike, because you found his apartment lousy with bomb-making materials."

"Yeah. How do you know this?"

"I had a near-death experience, and a voice came out of the Great Light and told me. Let me finish. You are holding him on that stuff, but you have *not* booked him for the murder of Richard Bentyne, because there is not a shred of evidence that he had anything to do with it. How am I doing so far?"

"You should be wearing a turban. But it's worse than that."

"What do you mean?"

"He kept a diary."

"Ah," I said.

"What, ah?" Roxanne said. I raised my eyebrows at her, and she realized she'd caught it from us and covered her mouth.

The lieutenant ignored the byplay.

"Matty," he said. "I love Cornelius's mother. I don't regret a day of our married life. But I must admit that from time to time, I am thinking about my job, or a basketball game, or what I'm going to have for dinner, rather than about the woman I love."

"Well, we knew he had it bad."

"Son, bad is not the *word*. *Obsession* is hardly the word. There is literally not a sentence in that diary that doesn't refer to his sister, how he wants her, how he can't stop thinking about her, blessing God for letting him spend his life close to her, cursing Him for making it a sin to do anything about it."

He shuddered. "In a way, I'm sorry I read it. I don't know—feels like it sort of soiled my mind. I've been a cop for a long time, and I've seen some gruesome things, but this is too weird and too different. I mean, the sister is a quiet, charming gal, and all, God knows how she fell for that Bentyne character—you all right, Matty?"

I stopped choking, smiled, and told him I was fine.

"Anyway, it's all in there. Why Bentyne had to die, why it had to be a bomb, why he had to send it to the Connecticut address—"

"It had to be the Connecticut address," I said. "because Marcie never went there. If he sent it to the studio, Marcie might get hurt."

"Exactly."

"But in the whole diary, the words arsenic and chicken do not appear, right?"

"Right again. Only in astonishment after the death. He was glad Marcie's honor had been avenged, but peeved he wasn't the one who'd done it. But how do you know all this, Matty?"

"Because I know who the other killer, the one who actually did for Bentyne, has to be."

"Ahhh," the lieutenant said.

"I even," I said, "know that we're going to catch him."

"How nice of you to include me," he said.

"Don't mention it. Of course, we *are* going to need some outside help."

"Your mission, should
you decide to accept it . . ."
—BOB JOHNSON
Mission Impossible, CBS

22

"Come on in," Clement Bates beamed at me as he opened the door to his room at the New York Hilton. "Nice to see you. What the hell happened to you, fall downstairs? I'm just about done packing. You gonna drive me to the airport?"

"Not exactly."

"Not exactly? How can you drive me 'not exactly' to the airport? Don't do me any good if you drive me partway there, does it? I'm gonna be standing there in the middle of the BQE, hitchhiking the rest of the way."

"I mean, I'll drive you to the airport, if you still need me to, but not now."

"Plane leaves in two hours, boy."

"Look, Clem." This time, I didn't even mind saying it. "We need your help. The police and I. To close the Bentyne case."

"Thought that was closed. Thought that was why I heard from the New York cops that I'd been sprung. I don't want to be hanging around. I'm going back to the grizzly bears. Too dangerous around here."

"Clem." There, I thought, I said it again. It was getting easier all the time. "We can't do this without you."

"Why me?"

"Because you were at the studio on Monday. But you're not connected with the Network."

"That's important, is it?"

"Vital," I told him.

"But I thought they got him."

"They got somebody," I acknowledged, "and he's guilty enough, but there are complications, as I'm sure you can figure. There's somebody else."

"Why don't your police pals arrest him, then?"

"They will, if they can. But there's a big difference between knowing who the killer is and proving it."

"Can't do it without me, huh?"

"The lieutenant is damned if he can think of a way. I can't either."

He scratched his beard. "I'd feel a lot better about helping you with a killer if you coulda gotten me my gun back. Can you get a gun in New York?"

I ignored his naïveté. I didn't believe in it, anyway.

"Oh, there's no risk," I said. "All you have to do is write a note—copy it out, actually. I've got the wording in my pocket."

"That's all, huh?" He scowled at me. "Is it one of those things where you try to fool the killer into giving evidence against himself? I mean, lead you to it?"

"That's what it is, all right."

He shook his head. "Only an idjit would fall for something like that. Where's the goddamn paper?"

I pulled an envelope out of my vest pocket. The contents had been carefully composed that morning by the lieutenant and me, with Roxanne and a late-arriving Rivetz kibbitzing.

My companion opened the envelope and read. "Dear Tom Falzet." He looked up at me. "Who the hell is Tom Falzet?"

"My boss, for one thing."

A grin spit the beard. "I can see why you want to get him, then."

"I won't deny a little personal satisfaction in what I'm doing."

"Good. Then I'll help you. I can't abide a hypocrite, but I can admire a little honest ambition."

He took a piece of hotel stationery and wrote. His handwriting was large and angular, not as old-fashioned as one might expect from a hermit.

I checked it over when he finished.

Dear Tom Falzet (it read)

> *Having decided that my being a man who minds his own business outweighs anything that might keep me here in this dirty city, I'm writing this note to tell you I saw you at the studio that day putting something in your boy Bentyne's picnic basket. I don't know if I'm the only one who saw you, or if everybody else is keeping his mouth shut because you're the big boss, and they figure to try some private blackmail, and I don't care. Frankly, I don't want a damn thing from you. I got all the money anybody could ever need, and I don't need any. For*

*all I know, you had good reason to do him in.
The only reason I'm writing you is because I
know that if I saw you, you might have seen
me.*

*Don't try to do anything about me. I am no
threat to you. I'm going back to the mountains,
and I hope nobody ever thinks of me again.
And remember this: If you did think you'd be
safer with the witness out of the way, I know
the mountains, and I am a crack shot.*

—Clement Bates

"Perfect," I said. I stuck the note in a Hilton envelope, walked to the door, and gave it to the hotel employee who had been entrusted with seeing it got to the right place.

"What happens now?"

"We wait until Lieutenant Martin tells us we can go."

"By which time, my plane is long gone."

I told him to relax. "I promise you a booking before the day is out."

We didn't have long to wait. We conversed.

At one point, my companion said, "You know. I'm still a mountain man, but I don't know as I'll be quite the hermit I was, anymore. Despite the poison and the bombs, I think it did me good to get out and mingle some."

I smiled. "That bomb was a genuine surprise, wasn't it? Anyway, I knew you were going to say that, something about coming back."

He was about to ask me how, when the knock came at the door.

" 'Bout time," he said. "Should I get it, or is it likely to be this Falzet fella with a shotgun?"

"You can get it," I said. "Code knock. It's Lieutenant Martin."

The bearded man opened the door.

It was indeed Lieutenant Martin, accompanied by Rivetz. Roxanne wasn't with them; I wondered if they'd had to stuff her in a closet or something.

Bates had just noticed that Rivetz had a scowl on his face and a service revolver in his hand. He backed up a step.

As he did so, Martin grabbed his wrist, spun him around, and put the cuffs on him.

"It all checks out, Matty," he said. To the prisoner, he said, "Frank Harlan, alias Clement Bates, you are under arrest for the murder of Richard Bentyne, and suspicion of the murder of the real Clement Bates. You have the right to remain silent . . ."

"We'll validate the final scores and be back
to announce our winner in just a moment."
—Robert Earle
G.E. *College Bowl*, NBC

23

You could tell it was a special occasion. For one
thing, it was the first time Roxanne Schick had been inside the Tower of Babble since she was a little girl, let
alone in the office of Tom Falzet, the man who had succeeded her late father as Network president.

For another thing, there was Falzet himself. Ordinarily,
he would have allowed himself to show the full extent of
his displeasure at my having used him as a red herring to
get the false-Bates to give us a nice juicy handwriting
sample.

As it was, he kept himself under control (the presence
of the largest single stockholder may have had a restrain-
ing effect), and expressed detached, almost academic interest.

It was only fair, in the face of such an effort, to give him an explanation, so I did.

"There really wasn't time to consult you," I began, "or, of course, I would have."

"Naturally," Roxanne said earnestly.

"I mean, the man was packing to leave, and there was really no way to stop him, without manufacturing evidence. I had realized that even if he'd been a hermit for thirty years and more, Clement Bates had once run a very successful company. There had to be plenty of authentic copies of his signatures in the files at headquarters out in Montana.

"Frank Harlan was easy—he had done a book for Austin, Stoddard & Trapp, the publishing arm of the Network. His handwriting was on file in the contracts department. A couple of faxes in and out—the lieutenant had the department's top handwriting man right there at the hotel—and bingo! Evidence. Bates wasn't Bates—he was Frank Harlan, who had killed Bates and taken his place about three months before he came to New York."

"Yes, but I still don't understand why you had to use *my* name.*"

"To make it work, we had to have a credible reason for 'Bates' to think we needed him for the trap. The idea of an executive as important as you, on a level with him as the owner of the mining and sugar company, made the most sense. And it had to be you, because it had to be someone connected with the Network—someone with an imaginable motive for killing Bentyne."

Also, I thought, it was fun to involve Falzet directly in one of these cases for a change.

Roxanne was enjoying it, too. "That was Bates's—Harlan's, rather—secret weapon. He had no imaginable motive."

She was superb. Kinsey Milhone could not have said it better. I would have been even more enthusiastic if I hadn't said exactly the same thing to her about an hour ago.

I picked it up there and explained how Frank Harlan had been a freelance writer, a successful one as such things go, but such things don't actually go very far. He made a living, and that was about it.

He'd gotten his idea for his book about the multimillionaire hermit, but everywhere the response was the same. No dice without an interview.

So he'd gone after an interview. He went out to Montana, and like Richard Bentyne a few months before, had started looking over the mountains. Bentyne had found Bates by accident; Harlan counted on finding him.

"Now he *says* he found Bates at the bottom of a rockslide, practically dead from broken bones and exposure, and that he died before he could do much for him."

"Do you believe him?"

I shrugged. "I think maybe I do. They've got him dead to rights on Bentyne, and he's confessing his head off. Seemed kind of proud of himself, the way he'd played the part of mountain man, the way he'd found the recipe for flourless fried chicken on Bentyne's home computer, the way he fired his pistol off into the woods to confuse the issue in advance, make it look like there was some kind of plot to get Bentyne. Other than his, of course."

"So, if he confesses to all that, I don't know why he would go all falsely virtuous over another one."

"Maybe they have capital punishment in Montana," Roxanne suggested.

I hadn't thought of that.

"Anyway, whether he caused it or found it, he had Bates dead. Then two things occur to him—nobody has seen Bates in thirty-five years, and Bates is the proprietor of a hundred and thirty million bucks."

I rapped knuckles against my temple. Mistake. It hurt. "Ooh," I said. "You see, that's where I went wrong. I kept

thinking about the *wrong money.* I got so bedazzled about
the forty-five million we'd agreed to pay Bentyne—"

Roxanne made a noise. "Heck, *I've* got more than that."

I goggled at her. I'd known she was loaded, but I hadn't
known she was *that* loaded.

"You *do?*"

"I love you for not knowing that, Cobb."

Falzet harumphed forcefully. He obviously thought I
was a schmuck not to know that.

With difficulty, I forced my way back to the point. "As
I was saying, I got so besotted with the obviously insig-
nificant petty-change paltry sum of forty-five million dollars, that I totally ignored, on the seeming fringes of the
case, a character who had three times that much.

"*That's* the stake Harlan was playing for. He'd decided
to take Bates's place. He was ten or fifteen years younger
than the dead man, but there was a rough general resem-
blance, and with a beard and a little while of roughing it,
who would expose him?

"He had plenty of time, he thought, to perfect his imposture, to figure out how he was going to ease back down
the mountain, back into society, and spend some of that
lovely money. He was already laying some of the ground-
work for that before he came to New York.

"Apparently, he had read some of the reports that
Bates's staff had diligently prepared for him over the years
and learned that everybody who'd known him at the company had retired and moved away, or had died. He was
going to take a couple of years to practice Bates's handwriting. Harlan wasn't sure Bates had ever been finger-
printed, but he was going to cross that bridge when he
came to it."

"Oh," Roxanne said. "I'd forgotten about that. Had
he?"

"During World War II, it turns out. Sugar and mining
for the government. Harlan said he didn't figure it would

make a lot of difference, since he didn't intend to buy an NFL team or build an amusement park or anything. He just figured to come down off the mountain and live like a king on the income off the fortune. Remember, he'd already researched Bates for his book. He was ready to chance it."

"He must have been crazy," Roxanne said.

"All writers are crazy," I told her.

Falzet, whose features had been a puzzled scowl, said, "But why did he come to New York? Why did he attack . . ." Then the dawn broke. His face opened into an "Ohhh."

Roxanne smiled at me and said, "By George, he's got it."

That brought the scowl back, fast. Falzet didn't enjoy being mocked in front of one of his underlings.

"You've got it, Mr. Falzet. He's sitting there in the cabin, eating his pancakes, made from L.L. Bean mail-order pancake flour, when he hears in the distance the whistle that tells him the mailman has just put something in the box on the stump. He goes down and gets it and finds a letter from Richard Bentyne, reminding him of the month they spent together, how impressed Bentyne was, and how delighted he is that Bates has decided to come to New York and be on the show."

"That must have bothered Harlan," Falzet speculated.

"It must have made him sick. He'd thought he was well on his way to being home free. Now he finds out that a national celebrity *knows Clement Bates's real face.* And he's the only one who does.

"Now, he can do one of two things. He can just walk away from the money, go back to being Frank Harlan again; after all, Harlan is a freelance writer and a drifter, nobody keeps track of him. His return won't attract any more notice than his disappearance did.

"Or he can brazen it out, eliminate Bentyne (ad libbing it all the way, he didn't know what he was going to find, after all), and then go back to the mountain and proceed with the original plan.

"The one thing he knows he *can't* do is sit tight and ignore the letter. Bentyne is liable to do anything. He might come back with a camera crew to see if the old guy is okay. He might do countless Clem jokes, send journalists back in the files, send photographers out to find him before he's ready.

"So Bentyne obligingly sends him, driven by me, to his own house, where Bates ferrets out the necessary secrets from the computer he's not supposed to know how to use. Monday morning, he wanders the studio, slips out to buy the rat poison, unless he's taken some the night before right from Bentyne's house. He snitches some of the flypaper he's sent the show in advance of his coming from the prop room to focus attention on the show's staff later, and he poisons the chicken, all before Bentyne has a chance to see him, or denounce him if he has seen him."

I paused for breath.

"Once again, he thought he was home free. But his whole safety rested on nobody doubting for a second that he was the real Clement Bates, the Man with No Motive." I shrugged. "Eventually, I doubted him. After that it was easy enough to prove. He hadn't had a chance to perfect Bates's signature yet, let alone the handwriting of a document of several paragraphs."

Falzet took a deep breath and squared his shoulders, like a man about to face an unpleasant task.

"Yes," he said. "The Network should come out of this quite nicely. That, ah, rhino horn business hasn't been in the paper today. Good job, Cobb." He saw Roxanne beaming at my side and added, "Excellent."

"No, sir," I said. "I did a terrible job. Because the fact

is, Harlan's impersonation was engaging and colorful, but he made a *lot* of mistakes. Mostly to me, and I missed them all until the end."

"Like what?"

I waved my hands. "Dozens of things. The first time he talked to me, and the last time he talked to me, he proved he was a liar about at least one part of Bates's biography."

"What do you mean, Matt?" I hadn't told Roxanne this part of it. Ashamed, I guess.

"First time, driving up route 95 on the way to Connecticut, I said that if he looked out the window, he could see the Sound. I meant Long Island Sound, but the phrase 'see the sound' *should* have sounded like gibberish to him, to anybody but a New Yorker or somebody from Seattle—they've got Puget Sound out there. But the legend of Clement Bates said he made his fortune never going any further than Helena.

"Then at the end, when I was pretending I'd take him to the airport, he made a crack about being stranded on the BQE. You and I know it stands for the Brooklyn-Queens Expressway, but would it mean anything to a legit Bates? Would he have it so comfortably in his brain he could toss it out in banter?"

I made a face. It got more embarrassing the more I talked about it. There must have been dozens of things, if I'd only been paying attention. I remember now he knew who Sybil was.

"But the big thing," I said aloud, "the thing that marks me as a total, complete and irredeemable idjit, as Harlan would say, is the goddam *pancakes.*"

"Pancakes?" Falzet echoed.

"Yes, pancakes. Harlan spun out a nice little fiction for me about how he and Bentyne had supposedly spent their month together—something, by the way, we'll never know, now—and he was always going on about how Bentyne had eaten piles and piles of those L.L. Bean pancakes.

"Well, no, he didn't. If he had, he wouldn't have lived to make it back to New York. I found out from Bentyne, just before he died, that he had a gluten allergy. He could *never* have eaten the pancakes.

"So I knew enough to expose the imposture right there, maybe even—*probably* even could have saved Bentyne's life. But it didn't register and Bentyne is dead."

Falzet harumphed again. "I know you have a big ego, Cobb. One has to to last in this business. But this is the first time I've ever suspected you of thinking you were God. Don't be so hard on yourself."

I looked at him. I had my suspicions—that he was being easy on me because he was just as glad Bentyne and his Big Contract were out of the way.

"The fact remains," I said, "if I'd been on the ball, this whole mess might have been avoided."

Now *I* took a deep breath. It was amazing how hard the next sentence was to get out. "Mr. Falzet, I want out of Special Projects."

Roxanne almost applauded. Undoubtedly, she had suspected I wouldn't go through with it.

But as soon as I said it, I knew it was the right thing to do. I was getting jaded and cynical, and on my way to possibly becoming a person I wouldn't like very much.

Falzet showed the salesmanship skills that had brought him to the Network presidency. He tried everything he could think of to talk me out of it.

And he didn't go away empty-handed. Somehow, he bamboozled me into making it an indefinite leave of absence rather than a straight resignation.

Roxanne held my hand all the way down in the stainless-steel elevator and across the lobby and out onto Sixth

Avenue (the real Clement Bates would have called it "Avenue of the Americas").

I had tears in my eyes as I left the building. Of course, that might have been because Falzet had clapped me on the bad shoulder before I left his office.

When we got to the end of the block, I tried to look over my shoulder at the Tower of Babble, but Roxanne said, "Don't look back, Cobb. There's a whole great big world out here to look at."

"Yeah," I said. I smiled and kissed her, and we went on, holding hands, home to walk the dog.